To H .....

x

Sue Hampton is a teacher who believes in creativity and discovery, individuality and fun.

This is her third novel for Pegasus after **SPIRIT AND FIRE** and **VOICE OF THE ASPEN** and she hopes it will make her readers think about the kind of education and future they want.

By the same author

'Spirit and Fire'
(Nightingale Books) 2007
ISBN 978 1 903491 58 4

'Voice of the Aspen'
(Nightingale Books) 2007
ISBN 978 1 903491 60 7

SHUTDOWN

SUE HAMPTON

SHUTDOWN

Nightingale Books

NIGHTINGALE PAPERBACK

A CIP catalogue record for this title is
available from the British Library.

Cover: René Magritte, The Fall, 1953
© ADAGP, Paris, and DACS, London 2007

ISBN: 978 1 903491 59 1

*Nightingale Books is an imprint of
Pegasus Elliot MacKenzie Publishers Ltd.*
www.pegasuspublishers.com

First Published in 2008

**Nightingale Books
Sheraton House Castle Park
Cambridge England**

Printed & Bound in Great Britain

To Philip and Sarah with love.

One

Lia and Sam were born within crying distance of each other, on the same winter day in the year 2045. Both heads appeared, in fact, during the same song. But from the first moments of their lives, they were as different as two babies could be.

Only one of them was technically beautiful. Only one was held in a father's arms straight after assessment, and only one passed that assessment with straight A stars. The same one: Lia. With her skin like café latte, her shiny black curls and huge cocoa-brown eyes, she looked, as her father said, quite delicious.

Sam, on the other hand, with his rather furry carrot-red hair and grey-green eyes, was not the kind of baby parents ordered at the Gene Clinic. And though Nina Simone was singing "I've got my smile" at the moment he howled his way out of the darkness into the bright hospital ward, there was actually a scowl on his crumpled face.

Lia burst onto the scene a few lines later, to the lyrics, "What have I got? I've got LIIIIFE!" – which meant rather a lot to her dad, Carl. He had been born in 2005, a few days after a hurricane drowned New Orleans, lifting up and throwing away the house that would have been his home. So he really hadn't started off with very much except life itself.

Carl liked to think that whatever he had, he had worked damned hard to get back. With money, looks and quite a bit of influence in New Britain, he was as handsome and smart as Sam's dad was scruffy – rather too scruffy for the hospital's liking. The first time the two new fathers laid eyes on each other,

George was shouting, arguing with staff who wanted to shower him, cut off his pony tail, shave his beard and kit him out in stiff visitors' overalls. And not long afterwards, he was angry again, this time about the newborn assessments the nurses had to carry out. When they tried to tell him Sam's first scores he didn't want to know.

"How dare they? On Day One it begins! Numbers beside his name, trying to shame him! Are they blind? He's perfect!" he yelled, red-cheeked and shiny where his beard had been.

George hadn't arrived at the hospital in the best of moods because the paramedics had refused to come out to the island when Millie started her contractions, so he'd rowed across to the mainland, his heart tight. Not that he wanted his boy born in a hi-tech hospital. But babies were not allowed to join the world at the Rainbow Dreams Community, not any more. It was illegal. Oh, the government still allowed people like them to opt out of the newly chilled, plugged-in world, and choose the squawking of chickens and the bleating of goats over pan pipes in elevators. But there were some rules that had to be nodded to if they didn't want to be chilled by injection and give up the wind on the hills for a white room awash with disinfected air.

No, George had nothing in common with smooth black Carl in his designer suit. But for their wives it was rather different. In between cooing over their contrasting babies, freckled and tangled Millie and stylishly immaculate Roz began a kind of uneasy but honest friendship. They promised to share the naming ceremonies they planned for the two infants, much to the annoyance of both fathers, who couldn't understand why.

So a few months later the families met again. Lia's naming ceremony was in a Town Hall decked with white lace, filmed and transmitted by satellite to the U.S.A. Sam's was on a rocky hilltop with falcons gliding above and the sea crashing below. Carl had been obliged to cancel important meetings to sit on damp grass and hold hands with long-haired strangers while a sleeping Lia dribbled milkily on his shoulder. His mud-soaked shoes were as expensive as his suit and just as thoroughly ruined.

Carl didn't understand, in any case, what kind of crazy religion these people followed. In America he had grown up in a church that doubled as a football stadium, where he'd tuned himself in to the rhythm and mouthed the words on the screen, swayed with the crowd and felt lost in it. He'd never felt a part of the wind-stroked earth or the skies where birds soared. In New Britain now, most churches that weren't gift shops or cafés were used by counsellors to heal the unchilled.

The day on the island was one Carl and Roz were unlikely to forget, but just in case, Roz filmed a photobook to amaze her city friends. Back in the comfort of their chilled, plugged-in home they could see for themselves the falcons glide again inside the movie album – and hear, as they opened the pages, the loud lungs of the little redhead.

But as time went by, the Rainbow Dreams community began to seem further and further away from their busy plugged-in lives. Roz didn't like it when Carl dismissed Millie and George as freaks or nutters, or ostriches with their heads in the sand. But she knew what he meant. They had made some very strange choices.

As for the ostriches, well, Millie and George had no plans to take their son back to the mainland that they had chosen to leave behind. In any case, George remembered Carl only as a smoothie with a very big if handsome head.

So it didn't seem very likely that as they grew up, the two babies would ever meet again. Sam and Lia, of course, had no say in the matter. Each of them was getting used to a very different brand new world, and neither one of them had any memory of the hospital ward or the very first song they heard.

But somehow, from the beginning, their very different lives were bound together in a way that no one could have imagined.

Two

At Rainbow Dreams there were few phones and no moving pictures of any kind. So Millie's only way of recording whatever she wanted to hold on to was to draw it, which she did, rather beautifully, on candlelit evenings. As Sam grew up, he drew too. His hair never changed colour, even when the sun beat hard and long on his slightly large (C grade) head. When his father George saw the resemblance in tone to shiny red lentils, he began to call him Pulse whenever he made him laugh, which was often.

Sam was sunbrowned and windbeaten all year round, still small, but sturdy and strong. In his imagination, nothing was too large or heavy for him to lift, and his parents, who dreaded finding him underneath a log or bike, resolved never to let him out of their sight. By the age of three he was alarmingly independent and totally fearless. Whenever he disappeared while their heads were turned, they usually found him with a young black foal called Shadow, trying to feed, hug or ride him. But to his parents' amazement, he never did get kicked senseless or cast off at a gallop onto rocks.

"He's a little survivor," said George, proudly.

"Looks like he'll have to be!" worried Millie.

By his fourth birthday, she had taught him to cook on an open fire, and to help bake bread and cakes. That was the birthday when Lia received her own pink laptop and filmophone at a huge plugged-in party where all around the walls relatives in America appeared life-size to wish her a happy day. Her parents had moved to London because Carl directed films now. They no longer invited Millie and George to bring Sam to birthday parties. Besides, Roz knew they could neither afford nor bear to be in London.

"We've got used to it," she told Carl, "but I understand how they feel. After all, they don't need masks when they step outside their front doors."

"Personally," said Carl, remembering the animal smells, "in that place I would have been glad of one."

But both the children could write their names on a birthday card, and Sam made his own. He painted a dolphin on it because he loved to watch them from his father's boat. Lia's filmocard showed and played her singing Happy Birthday to him in a shy but tuneful voice, complete with piano and strings. Sam reran it over and over again, insisting on one final performance even after a goat had chewed and spat it out – and the song creaked out of a sick-puddled mangle scorned by the chickens.

Perhaps at this stage the two children could not have sustained much of a conversation, but they had no chance to try. George said he didn't need a phone, even a no frills, turn of the century mobile without film, and he wouldn't be bullied by a government that dictated that everyone in New Britain must own one. Millie thought it was a shame to have to rely on letters which could only be posted once a week, and took another week to reach their destination. But she had stopped writing to Roz, because Roz seemed too busy to write back.

George also refused to own a computer, even when a government official came across in a fast, shiny boat to persuade all the Rainbow Dreams brothers and sisters that it was the law.

18

"If we wanted to be wired up and plugged into the world we gave up on, we wouldn't be here," George said.

"All I can say is that the time will come when you won't have a choice," warned the man in the suit, who was looking less than chilled.

"Oh," said George, "I'll always have a choice. The day I stop choosing will be the day I die."

When he said those words, Sam was sitting on the grass eating a carrot he'd pulled out of the ground only minutes earlier. He looked up at his father, because he knew what dying meant. He'd seen a bony, bedraggled kid born dead to a mother goat who turned her back on it, and found chickens lying lifeless in the dirt and grain, eyes still bright and beaks wide open in surprise.

"Don't die," he said, and his father picked him up and tousled his hair, as if it wasn't already sleep-tangled enough.

"How can I die," his father grinned, "while I've got a Pulse?"

But choosing didn't come into it, in the end, when the storm blew up wild and sudden on the very evening that George was returning home from the mainland. If it hadn't been for a very good reason, he wouldn't have set out in the rowing boat when the sky looked pewter-cold. The paper and paints were both running out, and he wanted to find a poetry book for Millie's birthday. So it wasn't the once weekly scheduled crossing to buy basics and sell Rainbow Dreams home baking and crafts. No one would have risked a sky like that just for a bit of money.

The old boat didn't stand a chance.

From that day on, Sam chose not to remember the lashing wind against the world, the drumming rain that threatened to break the glass, the white face of his mother in the moonlight, wet with tears, or the sobbing as she held him to her as if she dared not let him go. He chose to forget the body washed up on the pebbles, heavy and grey as a seal, and cold as stone.

"Dad!" he cried, the morning he found his father, face down on the beach.

He ran to hug the jacket and jeans which looked so familiar, but smelt so strange. Before he could touch them he heard his mother's cry.

"Sam! No! Come away!"

But he did not move. He watched his mother stumble down and kneel beside his father, her red hair beating against her face, her howls swallowed by the wind in the waves. Then she turned to Sam, lifted him in her damp arms, and carried him tightly away, all the while murmuring above his head.

"That's not Daddy, darling, not Daddy, not Daddy. He's gone, gone. Daddy's gone."

Three

So if things had been different, if George had picked flowers for Millie's birthday, or baked her a cake, Sam might never have seen Lia again. In fact, it would not have happened if Carl Harding had had his way. For him, Rainbow Dreams had become a strange and not very sweet-smelling memory.

But Roz would not be stopped. Millie, she declared, needed her whether she knew it or not, so she hired the fastest skim-cruiser complete with crew, and took Lia, laptop, filmophone and enormous blue furry dolphin with her.

So four-year-old Lia got to do something that Millie's parents had never brought themselves to do. She stayed on the island, in the Rainbow Dreams community, and bonded with many of the animals as well as the people. Most fascinating to her was Shadow, sleek and powerful now, but unusually gentle and patient. Seeing Sam sitting proud and comfortable on his back, she begged to do the same, but her mother only lifted her to stroke his head. She had never felt or smelt anything like it.

The blue furry dolphin proved rather less exciting in spite of the uncanny realism of its repertoire of sounds and its tickling teeth. Lia just wanted a glimpse of a real one, and had to be dragged away from the rocks at twilight once Sam's hand-knitted jumper no longer stopped her shivering.

In fact Lia had such a wonderful time on the beach, in the sea, and in the hay with the goats and newborn chicks, that if it had been up to her, she wouldn't have opened up her laptop at all. It was Sam who just couldn't leave it alone, until one morning when he turned it on after breakfast, his mother snapped. "Shut that thing down – now!"

Roz could see from Sam's shocked eyes that Millie never shouted that way. And though she was sorry, because she knew that grief stretched her so tight she was easy to break, she felt hurt too. Millie looked at Lia's laptop as if it was poison, as if it could infect them all.

Unable to explain what had got into her, Millie didn't stop sobbing until Roz put it away and promised it would stay in its case till they left.

Deep down, Roz knew that Millie felt contaminated. In spite of all the kindness Millie and the other Rainbow Dreamers had shown her, she felt unwanted and out of place.

Back in London she admitted to Carl that he'd been right after all. It had been a mistake. Millie didn't need her one little bit; she was already surrounded by love. What Roz didn't tell Carl was that she herself could count on the fingers of one hand the people who really cared who she was, underneath. But Millie had not only earned the friendship of every adult and child on the island, but appeared to be on pretty good terms with the animals too – which Roz found very hard to comprehend, especially as they had had no medication, and very few of them were housetrained.

"God, I was scared!" she told Carl, remembering the huge black head through the window, and the noise through the gaping nostrils.

It hadn't helped when the flowerpots had clattered down from the windowsill, spraying mud everywhere, but when the back door started to creak, Roz had imagined a frenzy of flanks and hooves, envisaged splintered wood and a six foot six panel in need of paint crashing down on the assembled heads.

"And there he was, leading it in, like a granny invited for tea!"

Though Roz felt glad of the government program to chill all domestic animals, this Shadow was no pet. And there was something in his eyes that was neither wild nor tame, but his own.

Carl did remind her that he'd said the visit was a bad idea. But there was something that troubled Roz rather more than a large black horse and a boy with no sense of boundaries. It was something that she shared with no one back in the city. The truth was that though Lia had always been an easy, placid child, she had never seemed happy. Until she took her to Rainbow Dreams, she had never seen her quite so alive. And it was hard, bringing her back to reality, to watch the life fade away.

"I miss Shadow," she said, but wrinkled up her nose at the offer of a simu-pony complete with sensory features, even when Roz explained that no-one could afford enough clean air units for a horse to gallop free.

Lia cried over the birds that concussed themselves on the transparent walls of the garden that used to be enough for her. Roz even caught her with her father's newtech drill, trying to make a hole big enough for them to fly away. And even after Roz told her that they'd die outside, she had the feeling Lia wanted to fly away with them.

"Where is the mud?" demanded Lia, another day, cross with the astroblend grass and obviously failing to appreciate the perfectly controllable sprinkle system.

There was a moment when the sight of her, struggling to carry a heavy panful of water from the kitchen to create her own puddles, stopped being funny in spite of the pink stripy singalong wellies and the grim determination on her pale face.

It was hard not to blame someone, and though Roz usually chose herself, the women were never quite friends again. But for the children, a loose and invisible knot that had always connected them had been tightened.

It was Sam's choice to remember Lia's giggle more clearly than his father's still, waterlogged silence. And over the years that followed, the memory of her warm breath against his cheek, before he too fell asleep on the sofa, became more real for him than the cold blue mouth open to the waves. And when he told Robbo, Lars and Henry, the boys he played with most, that his twin sister was over the sea, it did not feel like a lie.

Sam had plenty of friends to play with in and around the cottages that made up the community. Soon he joined the island's one tiny school, where he sometimes sat with girls, worked with them in the classroom or chatted with them over lunch on the grass. But none of them looked like Lia, laughed like Lia, or smiled with such wide, happy eyes.

As they grew old enough to write, the best day of his week became Post Day, when a letter produced on the pink laptop and scented with something sweet or flowery fell to the doormat. Goodness only knew what she made of his efforts – all big, scrawly and clumsily joined, but decorated with pictures of chicks and starfish and anything else he'd been practising. Anyway, if she thought he was dumb she didn't say so. She wrote as if she liked his letters as much as he liked hers.

He didn't know that the Lia who used to sleep in perfect peace had got lost somewhere. "In between worlds," was what Roz told a counsellor. In her place was a Lia who sweated through the night, and sobbed herself out of nightmares, cried when she left her mother to go to school, and often chose to be alone. She seemed to be faking the light in her eyes to please others rather than herself. Roz talked to Carl about therapy, but he was certain it was just a phase, just a growing up thing.

"I want Sam," she cried one night when Roz tried to soothe her into sleep.

"We should have another baby," Roz told Carl.

They took her to Surroundozoo, but she cried because Sam had told her the tigers were dead.

"Look how beautiful they are," Carl told her.

But Roz knew the tense was wrong, and could only kiss Lia's forehead when she said, "It's just pretend."

"You tell 'em," said a voice from somewhere, a young male voice with a tone Roz could not identify but wasn't sure she liked.

She saw a pretty, lush-haired boy in front. His shaven-headed father's glare would have melted metal. Glad that Lia, face buried now against her chest, neither saw nor heard, she was even more relieved when they strode up the aisle and out, the hostile silence broken only by a low and rasping, "For God's sake, Rory."

But Lia also wanted to leave, claiming it was "too sad" and asking her father to promise never to take her there again.

Sam never saw Lia to miss her smile, and knew nothing of her silences. In her letters he detected only life. They were neater than his, and more accurate, even when she didn't use a computer. She told him about her kitten, and how she called it Blancmange, after a sweet white pudding her American grandmother made for her when she went to stay. He learned about her new house and every amazing plugged-in gadget in her bedroom, including a panoramovision T.V. that spread movies around her walls, and could, if she wished, fill her nostrils and stir her hair. As time passed, Sam could only guess what she looked like, and how she sounded.

Then, a few years later, soon after they had both turned nine, she wrote to tell him that the American grandmother had died of cancer. *We had the same kind of heart,* she wrote. And Sam hoped he did too.

Over the next two years the letters became shorter and less frequent, until Millie was sure the friendship was fizzling out. Sam asked her for a phone, any old phone, to call Lia in London, but the answer was the same as ever. One old computer in each classroom and one in the school office was all the community needed, and a few basic old mobiles between them, for emergencies.

"Besides, Sam, there's no money."

He suspected that his friend in London had more money than all the RD brothers and sisters put together, but if either of them was envious of the other, it was Lia, who had never sent a letter without telling him how much she missed Shadow and the sea.

The community was informed that mail would no longer be brought across by boat, since this was uneconomical. What it boiled down to was that if the RD brothers and sisters wanted letters from the mainland, one of them would have to jump into the rowing boat and get them. On community supper night it was agreed that there would be a rota. Someone would make the journey once a month to check whether there was anything waiting in the part-time sorting office a mile or two from Greatport on the nearest coast. Millie was promised that they would never cross unless the sky was blue and the air was still.

Sam just kept on nagging. He could not believe that Lia would just stop, forget, and cut him out of her life, not when he'd been there at the beginning of it. When the boat returned, there was only one letter in Greg's pocket that wasn't unwelcome, official and produced by a machine. He opened it at once, and read it sitting on the grass, watching Shadow enjoying the air.

He had always been sure Lia was both clever and talented, and that her teachers must think the world of her, so he was surprised to read the first three sentences.

I hate school. I HATE it. I really, really do, and nobody believes me.

The rest of the letter, which was the shortest yet, grew chirpier, newsy, even light-hearted in places. But Sam just couldn't see her smiling when she wrote it.

Lia didn't know it, but at the same time she was writing the letter, less than ten miles away the boy who had unsettled her mother at the Surroundozoo was writing a song. Like most of the letter, the lyrics were committed with some feeling to the cycloshredder.

Rory swore, stared at himself in the revolvo-mirror and tried to erase from his reflection every negative imbalance that stared back. There was the downturn of the mouth, the steeliness in the eyes, the emotion that kept burning its way back between sessions as the chilling wore thin.

The face deadened now, in a vacant impression of post-chill Rory, he noticed the sweat that wasn't supposed to bead his forehead, not now that his dad had invested in optimo-balance thermoheat designed to make perspiration as outdated as shivering.

Rory flicked the control on his dad's old lighter and held the flame to the tip of the hair that fell across his forehead. Chickening out at the first pungent stench of singeing, he laughed at himself and looked around his room. The brush strokes that he had laid black across the walls to defeat the latest home entertainment technology were jagged and criss-cross. You could see the drips, shiny and lumpen.

Nothing. There must be something.

Rory, on his stomach now on the bed, leaned over to investigate what might be underneath, and pulled out a plastic toy his father had kept from his toddlerhood, its green face so ugly Rory was surprised it hadn't given him nightmares. He held the flame to the creature's features until the head melted like a candle, shiny eyes sliding down its chin. Its claw-footed leg felt warm now in his hand so he dropped it into the cycloshredder, listening to the hissing, watching the plastic clog the tiny holes.

It was his father's fault. No secret smoking, no lighter for unchilled son to look after. No lighter, no flame. No flame, no charred skin throbbing on his musician's thumb.

"Sorry, Dad," said Rory, "wherever the hell you are."

Four

Dear Lia,

It's Feb as I write but may be June by the time you read it! 2056, by the way! I haven't put my address because you know where I am. I'm not likely to go anywhere. Why do you hate school? Do you mean it? I like mine, and my Class Two teacher. Did I tell you about Beaky? She's really Mrs Bird, she's quite old and she was born in Calcutta. Her glasses are round and her nose is long and thin. Somehow she makes maths kind of fast and fun.

She'd have a bit of a problem with Games, but Mr Jameson does that and he's friends with my mum so out of school I call him Dave. I forget sometimes and call him Dave when we're doing workouts and Mr Jameson when he's round at ours helping Mum mend something. He doesn't mind because he's friendly whoever he's being. He's good at football, but we only play five-a-side anything because we can only just manage five people to make a side, unless we put the Early Years kids in the teams and they'd probably cry if someone like Robbo kicked the ball hard like he does and it knocked them flat or something. I've drawn that. It might cheer you up.

We've got two other teachers but one is the Head. That's Oddball, or Mr O'Dell. He sits on the computer all day and says he doesn't like it. Well it must be hard on his bum! He's a bit of an Ancient Geek! Mum says he has a lot to worry about even though there are only about thirty-five children. It's the paperwork and the money, she says, and the rules he's breaking. I don't know what she means. How can teachers break rules?

Miss Lane is the odd one because she came from the mainland, which means that to regular people she's actually the only one who isn't weird! She's quite young and hot. She wears make up and her hair is smart. Mum says she'll get fed up because there aren't any clubs where she can go dancing. I didn't know you can dance at clubs. Beaky does Country Dancing club but really it's another lesson because we all have to go or it wouldn't work with a handful of us prancing about like wallies. I prance round like a bit of a wally anyway. You'd laugh yourself sick if you saw me. Have you ever laughed yourself sick? I tried once but I didn't manage it even though I had the bucket ready.

Anyway the best thing about school is art, although things do run out sometimes. And I like writing stories because I like finding my own ideas, even though they run out sometimes too.

I still ride Shadow every day, sometimes on the beach. Dave says he's never known a horse so mad about water. I reckon he'd swim to the mainland given half the chance. So would I, if there was anything there worth seeing – apart from you. I hope you like my picture of a cormorant. I saw one yesterday. The falcon should be nesting soon too. I hope there are lots of eggs and nobody from the mainland comes to steal them. Mr Jameson's watching out like a hawk. He says they'll take those eggs over his dead body but I don't think people should say things like that, do you?

This is the longest letter I have ever written in my whole life. With paragraphs! Please tell me why you hate school. Mum says your school must be very different from mine. How? What is linegrading? Don't be unhappy. I wish you could see the dolphins. It's hard to be miserable when they smile at you.

31

Sam signed his name and grinned at the cartoon of Robbo and the flat infant. He was quite proud of the cormorant. He wished he didn't have so long to wait for a reply to reach him.

Sometimes Sam felt strange about being cut off from New Britain. He knew his mum wanted to keep it all some vague, alien mystery scary enough to deter him, so that he would never think to see for himself. And it might have worked, if this world he was supposed to scorn hadn't been where Lia lived. On the question of the phone, Millie wouldn't budge an inch.

Even in the Social Priority Centres where the poorest people lived, worked and chilled, phones were issued to every young citizen who couldn't afford one, on his or her tenth birthday. But they'd probably overlook Rainbow Dreams. And in any case, Sam Mcallister was impatient.

One day when he admitted to being under the weather and his mother was keen to feel his forehead, Sam wanted to know why they couldn't visit the Hardings, just for once, if only for a couple of days.

"We went to see Grandma and Grandad," he objected. "And we didn't die."

"Lia is a lovely girl, Sam, but she lives in a different world. It isn't ours and I'm thankful that you don't have to grow up in it."

Sam didn't scowl or sulk or call his mother names, but that evening he suddenly sat up in bed, put on his clothes and slipped out for a full moon walk to cool himself down. On the beach he threw pebbles, watched for the gleam of dolphins, and listened for their song, but the sea seemed to gather a steely silence around it, up from its depths – a heartlessness, as if all it was prepared to give was a washed-up father thrown away into the wind.

The boat was tied up in the shed by the jetty where it always was, with only a rope to hold it back. Maybe Sam was half-asleep. Maybe, as Millie had suspected at bedtime, he had a temperature that clouded his brain. But he untied the rope, climbed in and took the oars the way his father had taught him, erasing his mother's wide-eyed fear with another face, more imagined than real, smiling and telling him, "Go, Sam!"

At first all he felt was spray, cooling the heat of him. And the sound of the waves was reassuring too, so close did it feel inside his head. But there was a point he didn't recognise when the change began a new consciousness sharper and yet more blurred than the old. And it might have been hours before he felt it: the ferociousness of the wind's bite, the chill inside, and the dug-out exhaustion that felt as if there was nothing left of him, only the rhythm outside, controlling his body and brain. As the waves rose taller around him he saw himself for the first time, in spite of the darkness, in scale against the ocean and sky. Too small, too young, and too stupid. And yet, for all the closeness of home, something stopped him wrenching the boat round and giving in. Though each breath ached deeper than the last, he kept on rowing, even when the waves stopped thumping the hull and started to tower their way in.

He was wet now, and saturated by a shivering that was also fire. He felt heavy, too heavy for the wood's lightness, bobbing like a cork, useless as a toy. Sam's mouth seemed to tear open, and into it flooded not the sharp sting of salt but the roar and flame of something thicker than taste, something that filled him

33

before he could spit it out, slipped down like liquid and twisted around like hot metal, like glass under flame. And through the blackness and the foam, the underswell that rocked and threw him, Sam saw the sea he had loved rising and twisting like a monster. And he knew, through the tongues of fire, that he had been swallowed. The ocean had eaten him and he was Jonah now.

On a nearby skimcruiser the pilot saw the helplessness of the boat, thinking it empty till he caught the glint of an oar's last thrust as it fought back. He had tapped in the incident message and initiated rescue procedure when he froze, on deck, at the sight. A school of dolphins, glistening through the searchlight's beam, arcing over the waves towards the boat, threading a border of silver stitches that looped and intersected in a weave of spray and light around it. Nudging it. Escorting it. Leading it away.

The pilot had heard of such things. But then he'd heard there was an island not so far away full of greenies with no TV and no pubs, and he wasn't sure he believed that either. He didn't call it in. He'd had a couple of beers after all. He just deleted the previous entry, under the word *error*.

Sam must have lost consciousness at some point before he felt the boat grind into the shallows. Afterwards he remembered the torches and the voices sharp-edged with panic. And one voice louder than the others, wild with grief, a grief he'd heard before.

Millie never asked him why, and because he guessed she knew, he told her it wasn't Lia's fault. He insisted that she hadn't put him up to it; neither did she know.

And he didn't want to tell her.

"Shhh, love," he heard his mother whisper, and over her shoulder he glimpsed Sven, not Lars's dad just now but doctor, holistic healer, once a paramedic in New Britain.

Nausea overwhelmed him then, a fetid bitterness raw inside, a burning that ate into his breaths. He had to be told, later, that Sven had heaved from his stomach the water that had tried to kill him.

According to a medic friend on the mainland, the government had been trialling a compound to neutralise pollution, testing it in ponds and aquariums. Had it been too tempting to pump a little into a stretch of sea abandoned by the real world? Sven thought a freak concentration of the stuff had almost neutralised Sam.

"You see?" his mother was saying, her voice thick and cracking, as he opened his eyes again to a world that no longer throbbed. "It's the same sea. We can't protect it. It laps right up at the edge of our little world and tries to poison us."

Sven said Sam was just unlucky, that he must have swallowed a huge amount of water, but then surely, to have survived at all…they must be thankful. Sam didn't mention the dolphins, though he feared for them, pictured them bobbing dead on the waves like plastic inflatables. He might have dreamed them. And the whole thing began to feel like a night sweat, relived with and without them, with his father's face, his father's body, and Lia, reaching out to him through darkness.

He didn't tell her, not then. One day. If he ever saw her again.

Five

By the time Lia read Sam's letter the dead fish no longer glutted the stony RD shores and Sam had located through his binoculars dolphins live and leaping. His stomach had recovered and Dave Jameson was telling Millie, who really didn't want to talk about it, that he hoped the same could be said for his senses. Lia, who was hearing a different Sam, read and re-read before she composed her reply.

March 5th 2056
Dear Sam,

*Thanks for your letter which really did cheer me up. I think it was that poor flattened toddler! Tell Mr Dave that if anyone comes after the falcon eggs I'll fly straight over and help him send them packing. If only I could visit you. I'd love to ride Shadow along the sand. Do you think he'd remember me? I'm amazed **you** remember me! I wonder when our parents will let us see each other again – or if they ever will.*

Your school sounds really nice. You know your teachers so well and they sound like real characters. As for being allowed to write stories using your own ideas, you don't know how lucky you are. Not just plans for stories, or first paragraphs that never become stories! Not just carrying on someone else's boring start for a story that was never your idea in the first place, but whole stories! How cool would that be!

I'd love to do art the way you do, too – free and fun – even though I would never be as good as you. I don't feel like I'm good at anything – even though I do nothing but achieve objectives all day long.

I didn't mind school quite as much before, but it's completely different now that we've been linegraded. Of course living in London means we get to be the first to try out all the new ideas. How lucky are we! I don't know what the government said to convince anyone that linegrading would be the best thing since spacecruising. But whatever they said, it was a lie.

I don't want to bore you with the details of a dead old day. So here are the five worst things about linegraded schools. Actually I could probably give you another five worst things...and another. Anyway...

One: We don't have teachers. Now you might think this could be a good thing, but actually if I ever met your Beaky, I'd probably run and hug her. When I say we don't have teachers, I mean not flesh and blood ones with their own smell and their own way of walking down the corridor. We just have computers, one each, with at least three educators to choose from for any lesson. So you check them out and click on the one that suits your learning style. I'm supposed to be V (verbal) so my simulated on-screen teacher would use more words, but if I was doing technology or science I might choose the K (kinaesthetic) teacher who would demonstrate a lot and get me doing inter-active stuff. I can't talk to them and they can't talk to me, except about my work, and even then it's simutalk, not chat. I can't ask how their cats are and they can't say my haircut suits me – even if it does. That would be a distraction. Unprofessional. It wouldn't help me to achieve.

Two: We work on our own most of the time, in little cubicles a bit like the two we were born in – but no Nina

37

Simone! My mum still plays her music. Does Millie remember the song? Anyway, we have to go through a Health Check when we arrive. It even tells you if you ate too much fat yesterday. Then when you sign on you get your study scores for the day before, with a pep talk in big red letters across the messagetape. One day recently I got: DISAPPOINTING PERFORMANCE ....WEARY VOCAL (I spoke to the computeach without trying to sound enthusiastic). MORE SLEEP NEEDED.... INCREASE CHILL TIME. You can't escape these messages. They flash up any time, warning you, having a go. There's no pleasing them – not if you're me.

Three is Chill Time. That comes after the morning messages, which really wind me up so I need chilling badly. But I don't choose. It's all set up. It might be darkness and pan pipes, or sunlight and panoramofilm with a beach or waterfall and panpipes. It might be dolphins, but even if it is I don't love them the same when they're holograms floating around in soppy music. Or, if your chill score is not up to standard, you have to check in with the Chill Practitioners (nurses), who'll sort you out with tablets. Unless you've been making trouble, or getting worked up about anything (like how you hate school), in which case you get an injection. Lovely.

Four: Behaviour Police. They patrol the corridors and playcentres, and stand on guard in the classrooms when we're plugged in. We don't play outside any more. The playcentres are covered over, and escape-proof. We're on film every moment of every day. They're wired up too so they can feed in to the messagetape or the nurses. Oh, and they search us before we even get the health check. They'll take anything that might distract us, even a picture of a gorgeous film star (they took Will from my favourite band) or a football moviesticker. So there's no *real trouble any more. Even the angry kids, the ones who start off with no respect, just get frisked, chilled and plugged in.*

Five is Social Interaction. Of course, Sam, you lot in Rainbow Dreams do that all day every day without a counsellor to help. You talk to people, smile, laugh, and listen. What oddballs you all are! We, on the other hand, spend most of the day in a cubicle, and we're not even supposed to say hi to the person in the next one because that's a waste of achievement time. So once a day we're allowed to go to a big white room and sit down with the other pupils and suddenly the objective is to communicate. What a thrill! But we're not allowed to just say what we want, obviously. It's all guided and led by a psychologist who knows about our minds and feelings. And in case anybody gets over-excited about being with other human beings, the BP are there, all around the room, arms folded. I tried to interact with one once – by asking if he liked the new song by Harder To Fall, the band with Will in it – and he gave me a behaviour warning (like a yellow card in football) and a right scowl. I was only being friendly!

I could go on, but I promised you five. Well, Sam, how does linegrading sound to you? Yes, you're right – a real barrel of laughs. About as much fun as cleaning out your compost shed when a dog has made a nice big contribution to the pile.

Actually, I'd clean out your compost any day, dog or no dog, if it gave me a day off from my big, shiny Level One linegraded school.

So that's why I hate it. But – and this is weird – most of the pupils here seem to think it's a big improvement because they believe how much they're achieving and they feel so...yes, so chilled. Apparently most parents think it's excellent too, because we achieve such high standards, learn so much, and don't get the chance to behave badly. And of course a school like mine opens at 6:30 a.m. so it's very handy for mums who work. They don't even have to give their children breakfast.

Am I crazy, Sam?

Lia was about to sign it in strawberry pink, but she read it through first, and as a tear slipped down her nose to the paper, she watched it soak in before she scrunched up the pages and put them in the cycloshredder.

Sam didn't need to know. He wouldn't understand. How could he, in his busy, colourful school that broke the rules and let children choose, and be themselves? He didn't even have a television, not so much as a basic flat screen without smell or touch. How could he begin to imagine the complicated and ground-breaking delights of a linegraded school?

And besides, he was her real air. Except for those home moments when her big, scented, elegantly suited father forgot he was an important man and danced to his sad old music, the thought of Sam was the only laughter she had. Apart from the compulsory Comedy Hour on all channels, when the people of New Britain sat chuckling merrily in every house in the land, and that didn't count. When she caught herself laughing, something in her rebelled and tried to stop. The laughter that Sam meant for her wasn't scheduled. It was real and natural. So why would she want to send him a miserable letter that would make him cry, or kick something?

She wrote about riding Shadow, protecting the falcon eggs, and visiting, but then she finished her letter in a different way.

I like the new Harder To Fall VMD. It's wild and rocky and I'm often in the mood for that when I get in from school. Sometimes I play it really loudly in the garage when I'm sawing things. I'm making a little table with leaves carved on the surface, but it's got no legs at the moment. Dad admits we don't get enough chance to do stuff like that at school so he encourages me but tells me to keep my blood to myself because Mum worries.

I'm writing a story at home about people who break the rules like you do. Don't worry. You're not in it. The hero is a boy called Jim who's much more handsome than you! There are lots of birds and animals in it and one of the nicest characters is a blue whale. I could cry when I think how they've gone. The sea must be so empty without them.

No matter how hard Lia tried, she kept making herself sad today. She imagined the messagetape that would be waiting for her in the morning: REPORT FOR HAPPINESS TRAINING. Or just EXERCISE MORE TO INCREASE WELLBEING. What a misery she was these days. Perhaps there really was something wrong with her.

Something wrong, though Lia could not know it, was Rory's father's mantra. Something seriously wrong. He didn't have to say it out loud for Rory to hear it in his sigh, or read it whenever he felt his eyes on him, full not of disappointment but outrage. The problem that was Rory. In between, when the Chill and Pill combination kicked out the tangles, it could be okay. Father and son could function alongside one another when they got the chance, on the odd night when his dad was home and they watched the Comedy hour, laughing in something close to sync. It made his mum smile, anyway, which gave those dormant muscles in her long face a short workout for a change.

But she shouldn't get too happy, because they'd be moving on soon. They always did. It wouldn't matter what either of them thought or felt, not once he'd got his orders. Rory was sweating again. He hoped someone had thought to book him in for extra chill sessions. Soon.

Six

Nearly a year after the letter that was never sent, Lia did not have far to look for happy news to share with Sam. All she had to do was open her eyes to see amazingly tiny fingers ready to grab hers. She could use her nose to smell the distinctive scent known as BABY and use her ears to hear the noises that weren't really cries so much as announcements or wake-up calls.

Lia had worked out that they sometimes meant *Is anybody there? I am! Attention please! I'm waiting to be served!* But sometimes all they meant was *Oh! Air! Light! Warmth! Sound! LIFE!* She had a baby brother and if the scientists knew their stuff, he would be perfect. He certainly looked perfect. But if all went according to plan, he'd never have a serious illness in his maximum-length life. He'd be a high achieving, stress-free citizen who couldn't possibly fail, rebel or make any kind of trouble. It was in the genes and these days genes were big business. Her parents had paid a lot of money for a son who came with guarantees.

"Did you ask for him to be funny?" she asked her mother, when he pulled a face and peed up close to her eye as the two of them changed his nappy.

"What do you mean? Of course he's funny! You were funny too."

"No, in the interview, when you said what you were looking for. I'd rather he was funny than clever."

Her mother looked surprised. She took another nappy from the dispenser on the wall and waved a finger at young Charlie, who grinned back and made one of his noises that meant this was fun.

"Would you? But what about being productive – you know, getting a good job, earning good money? Not many people succeed by being funny."

"Yes they do!" cried Lia. "They achieve their objective of making people laugh!"

It was her mother's cue to laugh at her now. She cuddled her too, but only for a moment because Charlie thought it was his turn.

"You, Lia Harding, are funny *and* clever!" she told her, as she held her, and kissed the top of her head. "And completely different from everybody else!"

"But you didn't order that in the genes, did you!"

"Oh, you couldn't…there wasn't so much choice then. It was all quite controversial at first. A lot of people didn't agree. Your father didn't agree…."

"So why did he change his mind?"

"Because of your grandma. You know about her condition. She was a brave woman, but she suffered…"

"But it didn't stop her being a human rights campaigner, trying to help people who'd lost everything like she did. Maybe

44

if she hadn't been ill, she wouldn't have been so brave, so strong on the inside. You can't order bravery, can you?" Lia wondered.

It was all very confusing, and Charlie, who was finding life very simple, butted in on the conversation so loudly that they weren't sure whether he was really hungry or just cross that they were leaving him out of it. Roz took him into the playroom, chatting soothingly in his ear all the way, until Lia heard the grizzles give way to silence.

Of course, Sam, I know you can't order bravery and stuff like that, like shopping on the net. But I think babies should be who they turn out to be, not the way they're programmed to be. I bet nobody asks for a baby who'll grow up daft enough to dance naked in the rain, or work out how to talk to gorillas, (the few that are left, and they probably haven't got much to say to us, except thanks for nothing) but that's the kind I'd rather have. Back in the first few years of the century somebody special like that invented the crazy bikes you all use, to do your washing while you pedal around the island and don't use one watt of electricity. His parents didn't ask for a baby who was unique – and mad, and brilliant. He just was.

I'd like a baby who has his own thoughts and his own feelings. Not just a high achiever who gets a good job. Mum says I'm different, but you couldn't ask for that, could you, because being different means no one could program you because no one would know how. No one would know the ingredients cos it'd be a secret recipe. That washobike guy was a secret recipe. And so are you.

In any case I love Charlie. I think I was quite lonely before he arrived, because I haven't got any really close friends any more. I'm probably too different.

Lia stopped. Charlie was supposed to cure her; she knew that. She was so easy! But then how could she resist? He was enough to make anyone forget the more complicated things. She knew she had frightened her parents with her hare-brained scheme to get herself over to Rainbow Dreams without them. But then, if they would only understand...And how could using her dad's credit card on the net be fraud when she would pay him back, as soon as she could? It wouldn't have been necessary if he'd let her take his pilot and his precious heliplane.

Lia repositioned herself in the letter. Back to the loneliness, to no real friends.

"Just you, Sam," she said aloud.

Also we spend so much time at school and lots of people go to EACs (Enrichment Activity Centres) afterwards. I don't know what happened to just being with people, chatting, hanging, but I don't do enough of it.

It's different for you. Well, of course! Everything is different for you! I meant you couldn't be lonely. You're all like lots of families joined together in one. You might not have a flesh and blood brother, but all those people you call brothers and sisters are real friends, aren't they? And they don't think you're weird.
Do you ever want to be on your own? I used to think I did, but now I start thinking and that makes me sad. My peace and quiet is kind of made in a factory. It's shut in. Yours is out there in a real world nobody made, except maybe God.

The last time she had heard that word it had been used in anger, by her father, who in any case didn't seem to believe in God – or, these days, in her.

"What the hell were you thinking? I mean, it's like some kind of military operation, times and transfers and shortest routes – money no object, of course – but its no-brain fairytale fantasy, Lia! I don't know what you think you're chasing after, or what's so bad about real life here...and your own family."

She had hurt him in a way she hadn't meant to, and her mum hadn't really been able to calm him down with jokes about initiative and linegraded education being more creative than people said. As if she had ever owed any independent thought to plugging in, chilling out or the world of the cubicle with its all-seeing eye. The eye that had ratted on her, turned her in, refused to delete and forget.

But there were scenes beyond the on-screen logistics that were harder to erase. Scenes she didn't share with anyone, from a world she hadn't known and didn't want to remember.

Lia had been frightened on the aero platform, surrounded by suits in masks, monkey-mouthed in silence. It felt like a horror movie with the volume cut, or a dream with bad smells, mice scuttling in dirt, metal bitter in her mouth. Even the eyes red-ringed through the holes looked hard and dangerous. This was the world outside that her parents had hidden, the world to which she had tried, with her drill, to condemn the birds trapped inside the transparent cube where they were safe.

And the eyes were on her. Of course they were! A girl without protection, mouth open to air beyond disinfection. Eyes wide and starting to burn. Some military operation if she'd died before she'd stepped into the aerotrain, and never made it out of the tunnel up past the tower blocks! But she was more afraid of the passengers, and the heaving of the oxygen-swelling fabric encasing their brains. Even if she'd fooled the technology, the eyes on all sides would have turned her in. And Lia thought of the Magritte painting, and how someone should re-vamp it, ditch the bowler hats for masks and masks and masks, a writhing symmetry of masks, all of them framing eyes that were just as cold and dead and empty as the city gents of surrealism raining heavy through sky.

The hand was on her arm before the aerotrain could glide in, before she could choke to death, or look someone in those eyes and ask, *Where are you? Who?* Before she could shatter their silence or lean close enough to read the silver microbooks held in their hands like phones. And was this who she could become, without targets achieved and skills refined? Would she end up on a platform, red eyes in the dark — at risk and expendable?

"God!" again. "So reckless, Lia! No sense at all."

And she wanted to tell her dad that was it. That was what it made for her. No sense at all. Best forgotten now, her finger in the grip of Charlie, whose eyes were not raw and did not haunt her.

Anyway this letter isn't about me. It's about Charles Benjamin Harding. I'm sending you a filmocard but don't be too scared to open it because he's only gurgling, not wailing. Write soon and tell me the latest from Rainbow Dreams. Do you really think Dave fancies your mum? Would you mind if he wanted to be your...

Could she write the word dad? After all the words they'd exchanged over the years, Lia still wasn't sure that it was safe to write that one. She decided on *her boyfriend*, and hoped that was okay, because after all he was Sam's teacher too.

Charlie nearly got me in the eye when we changed his nappy today. I bet you did that too. Mum says boys never learn how to aim. And England still can't hit the back of the net either! Will you listen to the World Cup on the radio?

She signed it and put it somewhere safe so she didn't lose it before Post Day, but she couldn't resist testing out the filmocard one more time before she slipped it in the package. Then she went to the playroom to catch up with the real thing, hoping he'd been missing her as much as she'd missed him.

Fat chance! She found Charlie fast asleep and very full, his small hand still on his mother's neck. Roz had her eyes closed too, as he nestled against her, almost as if he were still attached the way he'd been joined inside her. Lia thought how funny it was that a small human being could be so blissfully chilled without pills, injections or counselling, while also radiating so much heat.

Seven

Sam enjoyed the filmocard more than once, but wasn't sure that Lia was fully prepared for the surprises that Charlie would be saving for later. In her clean, white, quiet life, all that noise and mess would be hard to ignore.

Sam's life, on the other hand, was full to the rafters of both.

"Can't you tidy your room, Sam?" his mum would ask, without expecting any action, or even any answer.

Sam didn't see the point. Plants loved his mother and thrived under her care, growing so rapidly that they were beginning to strangle everything else. The community's animals seemed to feel equally at home indoors, and even though he was nearly twelve now, and swept and mopped the wooden floors every day, the house still felt as if it would rather be outside in the sunshine.

The sink was never sure whether it was for soaking mud-caked jeans, washing up the rather exquisite dinner service that Millie's mum and dad had given her as a wedding present, or bathing a kid that needed special care. If left to its own devices for too long, the breadbin sometimes tried to grow its own fungus, and it wasn't always easy to distinguish the smell of home-made beer from the smell of sweaty feet, especially as old socks did get used for straining.

"Is Dave eating with us tonight?" Sam wondered, opening the filmocard one more time and grinning at the small, easily silenced noise from the tiny moving baby.

"Has that thing got smell?" asked Millie. "I love the smell of baby."

It was odd the way she acted as if they had forgotten it, his brainstorm, the gulps of poison, the bid to sail the seas in search of Lia. Millie was cutting up the coriander she'd picked earlier from the little herb garden outside the kitchen window. It grew enough to flavour the food in every cottage in the community.

"I asked first," he pointed out. "But no, and you can't feel his cute diddy hair either, cos there's no texture on it. Shall I complain?"

"Oh," she said, disappointed. "Can you keep an eye on the pan a minute while I get the washing in? And yes, Dave is eating with us, and so are Edith and Greg. Sam, are you listening?" she checked. "You forgot to look after the cashew pie last time I invited them, so don't get distracted and forget to stir, will you?"

"You don't have to invite Edith and Greg so I don't notice what's going on with Mr Jameson. With Dave," said Sam, but she was out of the kitchen door, singing as she reached up to the billowing sheets and towels that tried to wrap her up.

He wasn't sure whether she'd heard. She'd told him they were feeding old Edith and Greg for the last time - before they cleared out of the cottage where they had lived all their married life and went to spend their final years with their plugged-in daughter in Australia. It seemed a long way to go to escape his cooking.

Sam wondered if it was time for the ten o'clock News and twiddled with the button on the old radio, gave it a thump when it didn't respond and caught the phrase linegraded schools at the end of some report. It was a good job his mum didn't hear it too, because whatever they were, and Sam didn't know very much about it himself, she thought they were about as great as a shiny new nuclear power plant, a nineteenth century slave plantation and a McDonald's, rolled into one.

Remembering the pan, he scuttled back to it and scraped the browner bits off the sides. Oh. Still, he couldn't see Dave caring, as long as there was plenty of it and as long as he sat opposite the cook, watching her by candlelight.

He just hadn't seen it coming, but then, Sam knew he wasn't very bright when it came to that kind of thing. It wasn't that he minded anyone thinking his mother was lovely, because she was. It was in her own way, of course, with that hair, and those saggy, stripy jumpers that looked like they'd been made for a rugby player, and her open-minded sense of colour. But he shared her enough already. Their door was always open and they were always squeezing in an extra one for supper. Or three, or seven. And once a week at least, when the whole community ate together, he might not get to talk to her all evening.

There she was, back again, singing her way through the door, her face hidden behind the pile of dry washing. Sam had to admit she was singing a lot more lately.

"How are they, then?" she asked, breezily, tossing back her thick red mane.

"Who?"

"Our only plugged-in contacts in the brave new world. Still freshly chilled?"

"You're being mean," he decided, relieved nonetheless that she dared to speak of them. "I bet Roz and Carl aren't mean about us, and we're the odd ones, not them."

"I'm not being mean," she protested, and he felt sorry for the word because she never was. "I'm sorry for them," she said. "I'm sorry for New Britain."

Sorry, thought Sam, that her own son had not trusted her, but hurled himself at that world like a squirrel at glass.

She wrinkled up her nose and forehead at a bitter smell that had gradually wafted a path towards the doorway. Sam, who had a fondness for crispy black bits but would scoff just about anything, found himself eating humble pie.

On the other side of the island Indira Bird, affectionately known as Beaky to the island children and many of their parents before them, switched off the radio after The Archers and sat at her kitchen table with a mug of steaming coffee. She hadn't been concentrating especially well on that particular episode, however, because her head was still full of an item on The News.

Beaky had no experience of linegraded education, but should she meet the minister responsible for it, she feared she would be guilty of the kind of verbal assault that would make every "little word" she'd ever shared with an awkward pupil seem like a cosy chat over cocoa.

Indira was almost sixty, but she once lived in tight jeans, high heels and strappy little tops, and even in those university days she had her own ideas about teaching. In an early lecture, noting the words *targets, levels* and *value-added,* she raised her hand and told the tutor that there must be some mistake.

"It seems I have been mistaken for someone who wishes to study business," she said, raising her voice to swell across the hall, "or economics. In fact I wish to help children to learn, and wonder, to discover themselves and their own passions and truths."

The memory would have been sweeter if the lecturer had not retorted that it was she who had been left over from a different time. And that the twentieth century, with its bagginess and chaos, was gone and forgotten.

She'd only won by giving up on the mainland and applying for a job on a tiny island with one school, 4 – 18, which was unlikely to be inspected and where the parents were tree-hugging hippies who only cared about their children's freedom. Their freedom was hers. No longer a tense and tired outsider, she had found a world where she could fit, and there she had taught what she believed in (or fancied) for more than thirty five years.

Right at the start she had fallen in love with the sea, the birds, seals and dolphins, and then, rather more gradually, with old Tom Bird, who not only spoke the language of his feathered namesakes, but was also a whisperer who healed living things with gentle understanding. One of the founders of the Rainbow Dreams community, he was the only man she'd ever met who could match her in an argument, just for the fun of it.

Tom hadn't been able to give her children of her own, but when he died, he left her surrounded by so, so many of them, and still, even now, a few more to come. Along with his pushbike and his wildlife, his curries and his poetry, he'd loved his football, and she'd grown into quite a fan. Now that the World Cup was fast approaching, she was planning a curriculum based on maths but so exciting and wide-ranging that any linegraded child who escaped to experience it would probably think he'd died and gone to Heaven. Poor lost souls. How she pitied them.

But it would come. Beaky knew she'd better savour every victory, every new term of freedom, because one of these days would be the last.

Eight

July 2058

Dear Lia,

Did you see the penalty shoot-out? I can't believe it. England won the World Cup for the first time in nearly a century! At times like this I remember there's Sassenach blood in me.

Beaky's an unlikely soccer nut, so she planned this whole month of work round all the countries who've won the World Cup most. That's Brazil, Argentina, Germany, Italy, France, Nigeria and Cameroon. As well as stuffing our faces with dishes we cooked from recipes from all of them, we compared statistics like how long people live, how many follow a religion, and what kind of government they have. And how many people are still really poor. Beaky's right: it's a disgrace. We listened to music and tried out a few dances (how embarrassing) and designed our own flags which tell a story, then made them, and hung them around the school roof. I volunteered to do the climbing and Beaky let me. It was great up there. We've got no real mountains on the island, just the hilltop where the open-air church is, and the little one where school sits, so that was the nearest I've got to a bird's eye view.

Oh, and we learned about the greatest heroes those countries have ever had, and wrote them into little scenes of drama. And we looked at all the landscapes and climates and how much they've changed since the victory in 1966. Beaky had to get as much maths out of the whole thing as possible, of course, so we did more calculations than the pundits on the radio, and studied averages and goal differences and tables over all the tournaments.

Beaky is always saying how important it is, because we live on such a tiny bit of Britain, to remember that no man is an island. One of her heroes said that. (He was called John Donne and he looked like a 1970's rock star. You'd love him.) It means we all need each other and need to care for and understand each other – even people on the other side of the world, and even you mainland freaks!!!

Sorry! I got a bit carried away. How's Charlie? He must be nine months at least.

Sam wondered if he'd told her a lot more than she really wanted to know about school, but then she always asked about that kind of thing because hers was obviously so boring. She didn't seem to want to tell him much but he could read between the lines.

He realised he'd forgotten to tell her that Edith and Greg were leaving, opening up the possibility of new faces. New blood. Sam told Lia he hoped some family might want the empty cottage, and preferably one with a boy of twelve or thirteen. He could have said a gorgeous girl of the same age, but decided against it. She wouldn't be more gorgeous than Lia.

Then he folded the letter up before it got too fat and went to see Shadow, who hadn't seemed himself earlier. As Sam approached the slope beneath the church where the horse was allowed to graze and roam free, Shadow saw him – or smelt him first, maybe. He probably did need a shower, but that perhaps a quick dip in the sea would do. Shadow trotted over, much more

57

slowly than usual. Sam patted him and they head-hugged the way they always did.

"You okay, boy?"

Shadow just looked at him and he couldn't read any answer in those brown eyes. Sam would have loved a ride, but he sensed Shadow wasn't in the mood. He held out an apple he'd brought with him, a lovely shiny red one he'd chosen specially, but Shadow turned his head away.

"That's not like you! You're not feeling great, are you, boy?"

Sam felt his flanks, but he wasn't sweating so you'd notice. They'd been managing without a qualified RD natural vet for more than a year. Apparently Beaky's husband had been a real healer and a whisperer who cured horses with troubled spirits, but since he died, the vets had had more ordinary expertise.

Sam decided that anyone with any kind of basic vettish skills would be useful right now.

"I can't see what's wrong with him," said Dave, a couple of hours later, when Shadow was back in the stables and Sam had dragged him over to take a look.

"You're not a vet," said Sam, stating the obvious, "and you don't know him as well as I do."

"It's true no one spends as much time with Shadow as Sam does," said Millie, stroking his mane. "He always did, even before he could talk."

"But I don't know what it is you're so concerned about, Sam. He hasn't got a temperature. He's on his feet."

Sam shrugged. Rugby-playing carpenter teachers were not a lot of use at times. But his mum seemed to believe it, and gave Sam a smile that told him not to over react.

Sam didn't sleep as well as usual. Millie had given him a pep talk about thinking he knew best just because he loved that horse "more than anybody else." He knew he'd been a bit off-hand with Dave, who was doing his best, but sometimes it made him so angry the way RD brothers thought they could go it alone – and trust in God or nature or something. Obviously if they kept animals on the island (even just a few, being a totally vegetarian community) then they needed somebody trained to look after them. He was pretty certain they wouldn't try to do without a doctor on the island, albeit a holistic one. It seemed to Sam that the animals deserved the same respect and care.

When he woke, he felt tight inside. He sprang out of bed and almost fell out of the kitchen door, stuffing the bottoms of his pyjamas into his wellies, ignoring the drizzle through morning mist.

As he edged in around the stable door, his eyes adjusting to the half light, the smell was foul. Shadow wasn't on his feet any more. He lay, his breathing shallow, his coat warm and damp, his head tilted stiff but still, and even when Sam spoke, he did not lift it, or turn in recognition.

"I'll get help, boy, I will," he told them both, but he didn't know how to believe himself.

He fetched his mother, and Dave, and even Henry, because he cared for Shadow too, but none of them had anything to suggest beyond fresh water, and towels to mop him down.

"Somebody's got to do something!" cried Sam. "We've got to get a vet. If nobody will come out from the mainland I'll row over myself."

The look in his mother's eyes was a reflex, but a shock.

"Don't think for one minute I'll let you get in that boat! Dave, tell him!"

"That isn't it, Sam," Dave told him, "It's the money. We can't afford a vet."

"I'll ask about herbs," mumbled Henry. "I'll find…something somewhere."

He shuffled off, unconvincing, and Sam saw that Dave would have led Millie away too, would have given up, if he'd let him. He grabbed his arm as he turned away.

"There must be money for a vet. Isn't he worth it? Would I be worth it? Would you?"

"Sam, sometimes we just have to leave things…to be the way they will be," said Millie.

The slow and quiet reason in her voice was an attempt to calm him, and he tried to let it work.

"Please, Mum. Forget my birthday, and the one after that. Use the money you would have spent on me. Please try."

The smile she gave him meant *what money?* She usually made him something knitted, painted or baked. But then the smile faded.

"Vets today are not just healers, Sam. They intervene. They have to. You know how dogs get chilled if they show any spirit," Millie reminded him. "And injected too, against anything they can catch, to prevent infection spreading. It's a pure new world out there! Bacteria are banned!"

"So you're telling me a vet would have to drug Shadow up to make him legal!"

Millie nodded. It was what she'd heard. But Sam got tired of all the horror stories travelling third hand across the sea. Sometimes he thought the seagulls might just as well have squawked them on the wind.

"It might be nothing," his mother tried to soothe him, one arm round his shoulder. "But if Shadow's time has come, then it's come…"

"How can his time have come? He's only young….."

Though it trailed away, he finished it in his head. Shadow was only young, just like his father had been. Sam ran towards the cottage, glad as he raced ahead that no one was trying to catch him. But at the open door of his own home he looked round and hurried on past, stopping at the newly-painted back door of Dave's cottage.

It was wide open, the cat slipping in ahead of him. He brushed past her and looked around him, scanning the kitchen table, the woven chair, the shelves. There, beside a yucca plant on the window sill – old, chunky and basic but in working order. He slipped the old mobile in his pocket and ran back to his own house, where he shot upstairs to his bedroom and rummaged through his drawers.

There were more letters than he might have estimated, some computer-perfect, some handwritten and colourful, some still filling the room with fruit or flowers, and all folded. Searching through them, letting them fall to the floor as they failed him, he stopped suddenly and grabbed the filmocard of Charlie from the top of his bookcase.

"Not now, Charlie!" he told him as he opened the card.

There it was. He took the filmophone from his pocket and muttered the number at it, shocked at himself as he appeared on the tiny screen, tousled, his skin oddly white, his expression grim.

And there she was, replacing him, with all her black hair piled up on top of her head but just a curl or two tumbling onto her cheek, staring at him in amazement, wondering, afraid.

"Sam? What?"

"Lia, I need you to help me. Shadow needs a vet – the kind that won't inject his spirit away. We can't.....we haven't got the money. I'm afraid he's going to die."

She nodded.

"Yes, okay," she said, and disappeared.

Sam had to sneak the filmophone back to the yucca. That done, he ran back to the stables and waited there, sitting on the wall outside, going in to check on Shadow, lying on the grass outside as the sun dried it, checking on Shadow again, talking to him.

No one bothered him, until his mother came to ask if he wanted lunch. He said Shadow wasn't eating; neither would he. Shadow was drinking, though, as if he'd been in the desert all his life. He had to fetch bucket after bucket of cold water from the well, but it never seemed to cool him.

It was getting harder to watch him. That foul breath was weaker and thinner than ever. But the damp heat that burned from his body was so thick, so heat-wave dense, that Sam felt its power to drain him, his spirit as well as his strength. Every now and then the horse tried to stir his legs into some kind of movement, but they only jerked and stilled again, and Sam could see that it frightened him, this loss of the power and the playfulness that made him Shadow. The fear was in his eyes. It was even wide in his nostrils and the feeble, panicking cries that he forced out like an equine SOS. And what was Sam doing? Nothing. Sitting. Watching. Waiting for something that might not happen. Depending on someone who might have to let him down. Sam didn't think he could bear it much longer.

It was a long day. Henry and Robbo both came to talk to him but found they didn't know what or how. Henry soon got the message that nobody was interested in the part animals played in the Roman army just at the moment. Lars joined them too, and said he was sorry his dad only knew about people, not animals, but when he came back from the mainland he'd do what he could.

"Thanks," Sam told him, but without disrespecting Sven, who was an excellent doctor, he found it hard to sound too encouraged.

Eventually the three boys shuffled off, beaten by the silence. Millie came and sat with him in the evening, bringing his coat and a cocoa.

"You're not going to stay here all night, are you?"

He shook his head. He was exhausted.

As his head settled on the pillow, he thought, as he often did, of Lia and what she might be doing. It all played through in his head, scene by scene, as he drifted into sleep.

In a state of the art, brain pattern-aligned sleepobed, Rory's eyes were shut, but in the darkness behind his eyes he was wide awake. It was happening. They were clearing out again. New walls to black over, new chill practitioners just when the old ones were getting used to him and the doses he needed. And he'd never heard of the place they were going to, but it was at the end of the earth or somewhere close. And judging from the banging of cupboard doors, his dad wasn't that crazy about going.

Rory crept downstairs to comfort himself with something from the store of red label junk food he'd hidden behind the cleaning products under the sink. The News was loud enough to wake his dead grandma.

But before he had even reached the kitchen, his dad spun round with an accusing glare. How did he do that? Did he have some kind of micro receptors stitched inside his skin? It was uncanny.

"I threw away your store," he said. "And where we're going, you won't be able to replace it."

His mother nodded.

"You never know," she said. "A life like that might do you the world of good."

Rory stared. No point in asking. No point in caring.

"Life?" he repeated, eyebrows meeting in cartoon puzzlement. "What's that?"

Nine

It was late morning and the middle of a Class Two maths lesson with Beaky. Sam's concentration – or lack of it – had already been exposed by a question that interrupted his thoughts, but everyone knew about Shadow, and even Robbo wasn't mocking his uncharacteristic dopiness.

"Sam!" he hissed from his left as Beaky tried to involve him in a problem that would normally have got him thinking.

He looked up as an airy, high-pitched sound throbbed through the room.

Indira Bird saw the tiny heliplane before her pupils, who showed great self-restraint by staying in their seats and only craning their necks towards the window. Buzzing in the air like a noisy hoverfly, it landed on the field that served as a bumpy and somewhat neglected multi-purpose pitch. There it throbbed, sucking, churning the pocket of cold but sunlit morning air around its silver body and spiky, spinning wings.

"Class Two, please do take a look," she said, over the muted hum that faded into silence as the air stilled around it. "It's not a sight I've seen in my long life and I don't see why you should miss it."

Almost all of them were on their feet and at the window before she'd finished, the shorter ones climbing on chairs, and one of the taller girls lifting up the smallest under both arms so that she hung there like a big kitten. But Beaky saw that one member of Class Two had interpreted her invitation rather differently.

Sam was out of the door and heading for the field.

"Robin," she said, calmly, "would you be kind enough to run and fetch Millie McAllister?"

Robbo ran. Beaky put her head round the adjacent classroom, where Dave Jameson was standing at the window with his own group of teenagers, watching Sam draw closer to the plane. A tall black man in a white suit followed a slight girl, who emerged first and hurried down the steps onto the grass.

"I know," he told Indira, hearing the door. "It's his Lia."

Beaky hadn't realised, but she saw he was right. She remembered the man from the naming ceremony twelve years earlier. He'd been uncomfortable, out of place and watchful, but rather charming – and very inappropriately dressed! The girl was so like him. His fashionable wife did not seem to have come this time, but another man stepped out after them, carrying a case too large for a laptop.

Then the heliplane buzzed into life again like an angry hornet catching the girl's black curls in a thick bush of a halo as it hovered. Carl Harding tried to take Lia's hand, but she was shielding something white in her arms. The plane tore away, and as silence returned, the kitten jumped to the ground and followed at her heel.

"Sit down, now, everyone," Beaky told his class.

"Is it Sam's friends from London?" asked Lars, who had seen the photocards.

"Yes, I believe it is, and we'll find out in due course why they are here."

Indira Bird did not feel as calm as she pretended to be. An uneasy feeling in the pit of her stomach warned her that such a showy intrusion from the mainland was unlikely to bring anything but harm.

Outside Lia was running. Carl Harding, meanwhile, was carrying a large suitcase and in no position to keep up, but watched her put her arms round the red-haired boy who had been a lot louder last time he saw him. With some sadness Carl noticed in him something of his father, in spite of his mother's mane and freckles. Same headstrong will, most likely, harnessed to the same kind of futile float away dream.

Sam stood and let her deposit the kitten with her father in order to reach both arms around his neck. His heart was beating so fast he had no words.

"Surprise?" she cried.

Still he only stared.

"Where is he, then?" she wanted to know, retrieving a fractious Blancmange from an equally uncomfortable father. "We haven't come for you, you dope. Where's Shadow?"

"Sam, I'm Carl." He was focusing hard to pick cat hairs from the suit. "You won't remember me. I just came along for the ride. Let me introduce Guy here. He's a vet."

Of course some wordless part of Sam had known it, the what and the why, the moment the noise stirred his brain away from numbers. But it had felt so unreal that even when she linked her arm in his, it was like the dreams that had filled his restless sleep. A smile broke across his frozen face and the trance was over.

"But not a drug-pumping psycho," added Lia. "He promised."

Guy didn't look like a psycho of any kind. But he was staring rather openly at everything around him.

"Thanks!" gasped Sam, probably staring himself, but mainly at her, at Lia. "Thank you."

His mother was there outside the school now, looking strained and anxious, standing beside an excited Darius O'Dell. Once, long ago, he had been a pilot, and he still had his eyes on the fast-disappearing plane.

Carl was kissing them all on both cheeks. It took the islanders by surprise, and it also took time. Knowing her father could talk till sunset with little help from anyone, and noticing Sam's agitation, Lia had to step in with a smile.

She suggested that her father went in for a cup of tea at Millie's place while Guy went straight to the stable.

Millie did as she was told, and led the handsome man in the white suit, red tie and shiny black shoes along the path to her cottage. Never before had she been so aware of the mud and animal droppings that surrounded them, the muddles in her hair and the way sun, wind and neglect must have aged her complexion since last they met. While he stooped to enter the downstairs bathroom she boiled up some water and buttered some scones baked half an hour earlier.

Millie had worked it all out within seconds of Robbo's arrival with the breathless message. But beyond the shock, she just didn't know yet how she felt. They were proud of their independence. Being rescued was a new experience; it would take some adjusting.

When Carl emerged from the toilet, which did at least flush first time, he bumped his head, but that wasn't all she felt she must apologise for as she sat him down with his mug of tea.

"I know why Sam contacted you...I don't know how...but I'm so sorry he involved you. I thought...I didn't know they had stayed so close, the two of them. I thought the letters had...you know...dried up, fizzled out. I didn't know."

Millie knew it wasn't entirely true. Boys didn't climb into rowing boats in the middle of the night for friendships that had fizzled out.

"There's nothing to be sorry for, Millie."

He took a cautious sip of tea and she pushed the plate of scones towards him.

"Thanks." He took a bite and brushed the buttery crumbs away. "Delicious."

Carl was hoping Lia hadn't told the boy in a letter about the credit card, the timetables, the aerotrain platform. At least the mother didn't seem to know. But he'd never been sure they hadn't plotted it together. And now, here they were, adults dancing again while those two kids pulled the strings.

"We didn't want the horse to die. Sam loves him. But it's a question of money…"

"Don't worry about money. It's all taken care of. I just hope the horse can be saved. I don't know how Lia will handle it if it's not a happy ending, you know?"

Millie nodded. Sam didn't give up on those. It was something she'd given him, but she wasn't sure it wasn't a curse.

"They're two pretty determined kids we've raised between us."

"Yes," she said, wishing George was with her, and feeling alone and helpless in the face of this generosity from out of nowhere, from a world she scorned.

In the stable Guy had taken moments to diagnose the infection and very little longer to administer the first injection.

"We used to have a whisperer here," Sam told him, as they watched, the two of them.

"Never mind whispering. Even shouting in his ear won't do it this time," said Guy, patting Shadow's buttock gently after sliding the needle out.

"Will he be okay now?" asked Lia, watching Sam as much as the horse, but hoping he hadn't noticed.

"He'll need a few more of those over forty-eight hours or so. Depends how he responds. He's in good shape, I reckon." He smiled at Sam. "You've looked after him."

Sam wanted to be sure this Guy wasn't jollying him along with words he knew he wanted to hear. It was a bad habit adults had.

"It took a while to talk Dad round," said Lia. "I'm sorry we didn't get here sooner."

"I wouldn't have wanted to leave it another day," said Guy, "but I think we caught it in time," and the calmness in his voice reassured Sam.

"I don't know how you did it," he told Lia. "You know, organised this, persuaded people."

"No," she said, "I don't know either. It wasn't what you might call a piece of cake."

He smiled.

"Are you hungry?"

She looked round for the white kitten. Blancmange was standing in the doorway, glancing in with a look that Sam interpreted as disgust. Lia scooped her up.

"I've been hungry ever since we left."

Millie used the enormous teapot that came in handy when they hosted the weekly community supper. There was plenty of home-made jam, which Sam had stirred and bottled for her when the blackberries were everywhere.

If only she had known that her son had asked people she hadn't seen for twelve years to go to the enormous expense of landing on the school field a sci-fi plane that looked more like an installation at Tate Modern, she would have made more scones.

Ten

After a lot of discussion, Carl and Guy both slept at Dave's. Sam gave Lia his room, insisting he would sleep on the sofa downstairs. This he did, in the end, although he thought excitement would prevent him. The events of the day had worn him out from the inside.

The long, impromptu supper meeting had gone on late, and been a bit of a strain at first, especially for Sam. He, after all, was the person who had committed the unspoken crime of communicating with the mainland...and, worse still, bringing that world into theirs. Some of the RD brothers had been close to panic. But once Carl and Lia had told them everything, even the most suspicious had relaxed over home-made beer.

Carl had worked hard at winning them over. He knew how to tell a good story, even without a crew, set or multi-billion budget to spend on special effects.

Sam woke first the following morning, and passed the time by making a pot of tea and a pan of porridge. Resisting the urge to race to the stables, he forced himself to wait, and share that moment with Lia, whatever it held. And there she was, appearing in pyjamas and fluffy pink slippers, sleep-warmed and yawning, and ready to head through the dew to the stable.

When they arrived, just the two of them, running ahead to see for themselves before Guy, Millie or Carl were awake, Sam heard Shadow greet his voice even before he saw him. It took a while for him to find his legs, but they were strong enough to support him as he made his way towards them. Although he was slow and a little unsteady, he held his head high.

Guy, not so much dragged out of bed as pressurised by two pairs of eyes that watched him eat breakfast, borrowed some boots.

He confirmed that Shadow was "doing great" and gave him another injection. He said it would make him sleepy, but it might be the last he would need.

"He's a beautiful horse," said Carl, calling in at the stables later.

Fortunately he had brought a change of clothes and left the white designer suit hanging in Dave's wardrobe, between the bobbly jumpers and patched dungarees.

"I haven't seen one for years," he added, looking the animal in the eyes, remembering what Roz had seen in them and startled to find it himself. "Not like this. Not free."

Lia stroked Blancmange, holding her tight in case she ran under the stumbling legs, or fled in terror. She told Sam that the original Blancmange, doped up for her own protection and theirs, had been run over in London traffic. But she did not tell him she had killed her – by trying to give her the freedom that Shadow simply lived.

Lia was determined that when they arrived home again, Blancmange Two would be staying safe in the cube. But away from needles that numbed. Or stole.

The adults were talking now. Millie was sorry they had not brought Charlie.

"Someone put his great big designer foot down," Lia said, with a sideways glare at her father.

"How is he?" wondered Millie. "I saw the photo...the movie thing. I always forget all the names of these gadgets. I enjoyed the gurgle."

"He's very well, thanks, Millie. His mother thought he was much too young to come along, and you have to admit, Lia, he'd be a real liability round here, covered in...muck...from morning to night..."

"Trying to eat the rabbit pellets and chicken feed!" added Lia. "He's always hungry. Always."

Shadow was breathing steadily now.

"Is he absolutely one hundred percent definitely out of danger?" Lia asked Guy.

"Yes. He's going to be fine."

She passed the kitten to Sam and hugged the surprised vet, who didn't seem to mind a kiss on the cheek. Then she crouched down to stroke the calm black coat gently rising and falling, no longer steaming with sweat.

"We can't thank you enough, Carl," said Millie, dreading to think of the cost.

"Millie, you are more than welcome," he told her, with his disarming smile, edging carefully back out of the stable. "Guy's brother was videographer on the last documentary I shot in Peru," he explained. "Genius."

Last out, with a word for Shadow, Sam was closing the stable door and promising himself he'd be back soon, just to be sure.

"About the Incas?" he asked. "Machu Picchu?"

"Don't be rude, Sam!" teased Lia.

"You know about that? It's not on the linegraded curriculum, is it?" asked Carl, impressed.

"They're not linegraded, Dad!"

Lia's voice betrayed her scorn at his denseness.

"Of course not," he said, "but I have a feeling yours may be the last school in Britain, the only one that hasn't at least been given a Grade Three restructure, if not the whole schbang."

"You're talking another language, Carl," Millie pointed out.

"Bad language if you ask me," muttered Lia.

"Anyway," continued Carl, "I'd love to see the school - and everything else – before we leave."

"We don't have to go back yet, Dad!" protested Lia.

"I'll give you a guided tour," said Millie. "And you're very welcome to stay as long as you can."

Lia gave her father a triumphant look that said she told him so before she headed off to the beach with Sam. There they pulled off their boots and socks because she insisted, and walked at the water's edge, where the waves slipped quietly over pebbles and sank into cold, clinging sand.

"It's not freezing!" she protested, through clenched teeth.

"Liar!"

"We've sat on beaches all over the world," she said, "you know, the kind with coconut palms and sand that's almost white. The ones that are left, I mean, that haven't gone for ever. It's like they were designed for tourists with money, who just want to soak up the sun and the cocktails, and don't bother to see how anyone actually lives when they're not waiting on them or cleaning after them. They don't seem as real as this." She shivered. "Or as cold."

"Are you feeling chilled, then?" he grinned.

"In more ways than one. You know, they could scrap that whole program if they brought everyone here."

"I think that would kind of spoil things."

"Yeh," she nodded. "Bit of a squeeze." She paused. "Don't ever let them spoil things, Sam, not here."

Lia kept tucking her curls behind her ears but they blew back and around her. She looked tiny in the home-knitted jumper his mum had lent her, and thin drainpipe jeans tapering into the small bare feet. He wanted to tell her his life wasn't perfect, but somehow he knew she wouldn't want to listen. He looked away, across the sea to the hazy grey mound that was the mainland, then back to the thin, veiling waves that washed over their toes and broke harmlessly against their ankles. Then as he turned towards Lia once more he saw she was waiting.

"Promise."

"Course!"

As he looked away again, he felt her hand on his arm.

"No, Sam, really. Promise."

He nodded, though he didn't understand, not really. He just knew how much it meant to her.

"Okay, I promise!"

It seemed to satisfy her, for now. Suddenly she wanted to build a sandcastle and it took an hour or more, with moats and battlements, slit windows for the archers to fire their arrows through, and a drawbridge that refused to cross the moat without melting into it. She talked almost constantly and smiled so much that Sam doubted whether Charlie could have enjoyed it more.

"You must think I'm a lunatic," she told him, when they had finished. "But I'm just glad to be here."

"I know," he said, then grinned. "Still," he added, "it might be a good idea to take a few more tablets!"

He ran back to the cottage with Lia chasing after him.

Eleven

When Dave Jameson woke to find his bedroom thick with expensive designer smells for the third nose-tickling time, he couldn't help feeling a different kind of irritation. Carl Bigshot Harding was a likeable enough guy, if you could forgive the namedropping. After all, it must impress just about everyone on the planet except those living in a Hollywood-free zone like theirs.

The vet was okay. All he wanted to do when he wasn't treating horses or polishing off home-baked cake was sleep.

But where to start with Carl! He took an annoyingly long time in the bathroom, washing off every trace of real, earthy air. He couldn't seem to accept that there really wasn't any whisky on the island, anywhere, and he was better at talking than listening. But Dave had to admit that he wasn't totally closed in like a lot of the politicians and high-powered businessmen he said he knew. He didn't want what the community had to offer, but he could at least begin to understand it – and that gave him an advantage over Dave, because for the life of him he couldn't think why anyone who stayed on the island would want to leave.

Dave himself had only checked out the job at the school because his favourite uncle lived in Greatport. Next thing he knew he was giving up goal opportunities in Sunday League matches to muck out chickens and hammer nails between marking books. He'd never been sorry.

And now that he'd grown so close to Millie McAllister, he knew he could never think of being anywhere else. He'd begun by wanting to help her, but found himself hoping recently that she might be ready to be loved again. Sam was another matter. They got on fine, but he didn't kid himself that the boy was looking for another dad. He'd seemed so steady before the incident with the boat, but then loss did strange things to solid people.

Dave dragged himself through the perfumed room, spluttering more than necessary, to find the bathroom billowing with scented steam.

"Millie will have made porridge by now if you want to go on over. Don't wait for me!" he called downstairs, flinging the windows wide open.

He'd forgotten about a sleeping Guy, but judging by the snoring from the small second bedroom, he need not have worried about disturbing him. Dave would welcome some time on his own – if Carl had left him any hot water. He didn't seem to understand that solar energy was only unlimited if the sun didn't hide all day behind grey cloud.

"As a matter of fact, Dave, I kind of wanted a word..." called up the big deep voice.

Poser, thought Dave? Would that do? Unwanted guest would be two. But he took the hint and scuttled down. It wouldn't do to keep an important man waiting.

"You got yourself coffee?" he asked, knowing there was no way Carl would negotiate his way round his slightly disorganised kitchen without an au pair or housekeeper to do it for him.

"Er, no, it's okay. I'll wait. Look, do you want to sit down?"

Er, yes, I will, seeing as it's my kitchen, thought Dave, sitting obligingly, and flicking a crumb across the table.

"It's about what I do. Make documentaries, that is. Among other projects of course. I've been very slow to see it – crazily dumb ass slow, in fact – but we're sitting in the middle of a show that no one else has thought about making."

"A show?"

Dave's memories of shows were not good ones. Reality T.V. that sank below toilet level, quizzes that required the intellect of a pigeon....

"A documentary about Rainbow Dreams – day to day, honest, warts and all, but no bias or prejudice of any kind. Telling it like it is, you know? No enormous crew, just hand-held cameras, keeping it simple without too much intrusion. And you guys could vet the script, because of course I'd want you to be happy. What do you think?"

"Why?"

Carl looked quite thrown for a moment. Dave supposed he didn't usually make this kind of proposal over a scarred and grooved old kitchen table that still carried the evidence of the last meal eaten on it.

But then this wasn't the kind of pitch that he himself was used to either, so he didn't know why he felt such a need to score.

"Why?" echoed Carl. "Why do I want to make it? Why do I want you to be happy? Sorry, Dave, I don't know what you're asking me to justify."

"I'm asking you why you want to put edited scenes from our real lives into people's homes. As entertainment? To educate them? To make them feel grateful for everything they've got that we've given up? To win an award at a glitzy ceremony? To convert a few more nutters out there who might want to come and join us? Or just to show your daughter that you care?"

As Dave spoke he felt the air grow thick with something more difficult to clear than aftershave, and the silence that followed told him that Carl felt it too.

"If you want to talk to the community about this idea," Dave added, "you'd better be prepared for questions like that. I'm no leader. I didn't even come here for the ideology. But I would guess nobody's going to leap up and down with excitement about being on the telly (if you still call it that) and you're going to have to convince us of your motives. If you know what they are."

"Yes," said Carl, slowly, nodding. "I see what you're saying. I guess I haven't explained as clearly as I should have, Dave. I hope you'll give me a chance to try again."

"It's not up to me."

"No, but I wanted to sound you out. And you've been very frank. Thanks for that."

"You're welcome," Dave told him, trying a smile to ease out his own grumpiness, but it didn't really work.

Carl was ready for breakfast now, even that sugarless, saltless porridge that tasted so strangely comforting after a broken night's sleep. Every night so far the wind had attacked and shaken everything around him, indoors and out. Although, unlike Dave, he smiled a lot at Millie's, as he chatted over endless tea, he felt unusually rattled himself.

Millie sensed that something had happened between the two men, because neither one of them addressed anything he said to the other. She put it down to Dave's awkwardness. Carl was such a gentleman. There was something elegant about his manners as well as his appearance, and his voice, apart from the enduring American twang, was resonant enough for Shakespeare. But which flawed hero would suit him best? Othello? Macbeth?

"I suppose you do know it's Monday," she reminded Sam, as she suddenly remembered herself. "Lia, will you be happy to go to school?"

Sam looked at her expectantly. He was more than happy to take her.

"Yes, sure," she said. "I want to meet Beaky properly."

"Your dad might want you to make notes," said Dave.

"I've seen the school, remember," said Carl. "Millie showed me round."

"Real cute, is it?" wondered Dave, who was finding it hard to help himself now that Millie was smiling so brightly at Carl and fussing over him as if he hadn't had a good meal for a week.

"Well, as an American with a slightly different understanding of that word, I'd have to say it was my guide who was cute."

This time Lia looked as cross with her father as Dave did. Even Sam was picking up on the undercurrent now, and shot his mother a protective glance, but she didn't seem too outraged.

"We don't do flirting here," said Dave. "You might say it's one of the many things we left behind on the mainland."

"Well I might say that's a real pity," said Carl, so confidently, so warmly, and with such a wide smile for Millie, that Sam thought it was a good job he was Lia's dad. Otherwise he might have trouble forgiving him.

It was the same kind of trouble that Rory experienced whenever he looked at his father on the journey across a grey sea from Greatport. And again on arrival on a remote island where the only net anyone ever used was not on screen but over gooseberries. Forgiving him. This time he wasn't sure he could even start. And that was before the animal shit and the mud, the wind that wasn't subject to temperature control and the cottage that sprouted like an old potato.

Rory scowled at his father and his silly clothes and hair, trying to look the part. Well, he might be able to fool those dopey hippies who had greeted them like long-lost relatives, but fitting in wasn't on the agenda as far as Rory was concerned.

"You don't look a day younger," he told his father, "considering you've brought us back in time."

The way his father looked at him, he supposed he might have been happier if he had – to a time before his only beloved son was born.

Twelve

Lia had a great day at school. She found Beaky funny and inspiring as well as real. She wished the art lesson could have lasted longer than a whole afternoon, and she enjoyed chatting with Sam's friends, especially the boys she'd heard about in letters. Robbo loved the attention because he didn't normally talk to girls very much, unless they spoke the language of football. Henry teased him for the rest of the day about the blushing.

"What do you like best about being here?" Lia wanted to know.

"I like the mud," announced Robbo, grinning.

"Well you're in the right place!" she laughed, and asked Henry the same question, because he'd kept very quiet but she knew Sam thought he was brainy.

"I like being a part of something that's smaller and friendlier than anything on the mainland, but also in touch with something bigger, too. The earth, nature, growing and making." He paused. "And having time, you know?" He looked at Lia. "I bet you feel like you've lost all that."

"Yes," she said, "and most people don't even bother to look for it."

"Henry," said Sam, "You're a walking conversation stopper!"

Robbo slapped him on the back as if he'd scored a goal.

"What you said is kind of what I meant about the mud," he said.

Lia laughed out loud.

But not everyone smiled, even at Lia. As far as Sam could see, Rory Fielder didn't do smiles. Which was maybe just as well, because he was pretty, in a moody sort of way. Dave said he had attitude. He was fifteen and tall and wiry, with long, dark curls. He had been on the island a few days now, and was being shown round the school, which included being introduced in Class Two even though he would be in Dave's.

"Where do you come from, Rory?" asked Beaky.

"You wouldn't know it. It's a town."

"I understand there are communities in towns. It must be very hard. We're so privileged here."

Rory raised thick eyebrows. Sam supposed he was trying to look sardonic, but Beaky wouldn't appreciate his manners.

"If you say so."

"Your father is an electrician, I understand?"

Rory nodded.

"Is he looking for an easy life?" wondered Henry.

"What?" asked Rory, taken aback, as if he'd been insulted.

89

"I think Henry meant there's a lot less work for electricians here than on the mainland, but of course we're not totally independent of it, for all the green energy we've cultivated here. I'm sure your father will make a valuable contribution, as a person as well as an electrician," said Beaky. "And your mother?"

"She's a shrink. Specialises in head cases."

"Ah. A psychiatrist – very interesting. I hope to meet her soon."

"She reckons she'll have her work cut out," said Rory.

"If what you say is true," said Beaky, the smile contradicted by the set of the lips, "she'll be disappointed. At Rainbow Dreams our minds are a great deal healthier than our finances."

Sam enjoyed watching Rory digest that one. He reckoned Beaky was ahead on points, and Rory didn't like it.

As she turned away he found himself looking at Rory longer than he intended, and saw him make a straight, tight gun of two fingers, fire it at the back of Beaky's head with a silent puff and then turn the barrel to his mouth to blow the smoke away. He slid the imaginary weapon into a holster on his hip, patted it and released a slow-burning smile that seemed to be entirely for the benefit of his reluctant audience of one. And Sam had to wait, had to hold eye contact as long as he could bear it, before looking away.

They were spared for a while after that: both the over-acted mime and the razor-sharp wit, but the new boy did offer up an observation on Lia's 3D collage representing anger, which was "awesome." Not that it was for everyone to hear. Sam saw the way he murmured it for her ears only as he walked past.

Lia did think he was unbelievably beautiful, but that was something she confided only to Sam, and then wished she hadn't. He frowned.

"More like a beast."

Sam's own collage was about sadness, and if making him sadder when he looked at it made it a success, then it worked. He had been feeling overwhelmed since breakfast by things he couldn't control: Carl behaving like some kind of smarmy Casanova with his mother, and Dave spoiling for a fight when he was usually so easy-going, in school and out.

Then there was Lia, who was only being her normal, friendly self, first with his mates and now with this pretty boy who looked like he should cavort with an electric guitar or model jeans in a teen magazine. He didn't know why it all made him so miserable.

Worst of all, he knew it was only a matter of hours before she would be leaving. There was no need, it seemed, to stay. Shadow was trotting now. He looked like he'd gallop any day if only someone gave him the freedom to try, and Sam had plans to be that someone.

He couldn't talk to Lia at school, not properly, and even if they managed a few moments to themselves later on, he wouldn't know where to begin. It seemed so stupid to have to wait for a letter to tell her stuff.

When it came, the decision to go, he heard it from Sleepyhead Guy, stumbling out of bed as they returned from school. The heliplane would be returning for them late that evening, he said, after a meeting of some kind. Then he yawned and stretched repeatedly and wondered whether there was any chance of coffee.

"The meeting – what's it for?" asked Sam, looking for a clean mug.

"Carl has something to ask the …..do you have elders? The leaders of Rainbow Dreams. "

"We don't have leaders either. What does he want to ask?"

"Oh, not my bag, Sam. Ask Lia."

Lia was frowning, as if she didn't know what was going on any more than Sam did.

"I didn't even know about leaving tonight. He doesn't ask my opinion." She grinned. "Although sometimes I give it anyway."

Sam couldn't return the grin, not in any half-natural way.

"I thought we might have another day, before you left," he said, trying not to sound too crestfallen. "Do you want to say goodbye to Shadow?"

"Of course I do."

"No galloping along the beach to show off to Lia!" warned a yawning Guy, as they forced themselves into boots. "He's not a hundred percent yet. You've got to be patient."

Moments later, as they scooped out some oats and found a few fallen apples for him, Lia laughed about the hard-working, business-like vet who had turned into a layabout after a few days on the island.

"The fresh air must be knocking him cold," she said.

"It's cold, but it's not that fresh. We're not inside a bubble, you know. The pollution you create on the mainland can find its way here without a map," he pointed out, grumpier than he meant to be, and more accusing.

There was an acid memory in his throat to back him up, but now was not the time.

"You talk as if it's my fault," she said, and he knew he'd hurt her. "You've been moody with me all day. I don't know what I've done. You know I don't belong here. You know what my life is like. I'm part of everything you hate – but that's no reason..."

Now she was starting to cry. It was something Sam hadn't seen before and it made him feel more wretched than he could bear.

"I'm sorry, Lia. It's not your fault, nothing is. I just...I wish you could stay....a bit longer."

"So do I," she said, wiping her nose. "I love it here. But then I miss Mum, and Charlie. They'll be missing me. I've got a home and it so happens it's just a little bit different from yours."

Sam felt stupid now. What was the matter with him? Of course she was going back. He'd made her cry for nothing and now he didn't know what to say.

"Come on, then," she said, picking up the bucket of water.

"Sorry," he mumbled.

"Don't say it again," she told him. "It's okay. I'll miss you too."

Shadow greeted them with something close to his old friskiness and noise, and was hungrier than he'd been for a week. He seemed happy enough to stand still while they groomed, patted, stroked and admired him, but grew fidgety with energy, so Sam led him out of the stable into the open air, and they watched him trotting into a canter, expressing his pleasure for all to hear, through his nose.

"I can't tell you," began Sam. "You saved him."

"You've said thank you," she reminded him. "More than once." She smiled. "What I did, well…I could, that's all. I've got the money and connections. You've got…." She said looking all around her. "…all this. And the world's most beautiful horse."

Sam couldn't argue with that. Shadow was heading towards them now. He put his arms round his neck and asked him if he fancied a ride. Then he held him still while Lia, who was silent with nervous excitement but showed no hesitation at all, climbed up onto his back. It was all they dared, without saddle, bridle or adult, but it was enough to light her up before she slid off again and murmured words of love into the horse's ear as she handed him back.

"Next time you come," he said, "you can climb up behind me, if you hold on tight – and we'll gallop along the beach."

Her eyes widened at that.

"That would be amazing!" she cried, hands clasped together, just as he remembered, when the hands were smaller. "But you don't have to bribe me, you know. I don't need an incentive. I'll come back."

He grinned.

"Okay. I believe you."

"You'd better."

"I tried to visit you once," he said, "but I nearly drowned. And poisoned myself." She was looking at him with a smile that obliged him to put her straight. "It wasn't my finest hour."

He told her about the dolphins, even though when he tried to conjure them up it felt so much like a dream he was amazed by her belief. Simple and total. It made him smile himself.

"I tried to visit you too," she told him, as they reached the stable, "but I scared myself as well as my parents. I'm not as smart as I think I am sometimes." She shuddered inside, the eyes on the platform gathering. "Not my finest hour either."

But this is, thought Sam, stroking Shadow slowly behind the ears. He did not see Rory, framed for a moment in the stable doorway, blow Lia a dandelion clock of a kiss. It was tossed lightly from the outstretched palm of his hand before he slipped silently away. The laugh that followed was a private one shared only with the chickens.

Lia and Sam wandered back to the cottage a while later to find Millie at Garth and Faye's cottage, helping to prepare the supper for the whole community plus departing guests.

Sam wanted to ask Dave about the meeting, but he was still at school. And clearly Lia knew nothing about her father's plans. It had occurred to Sam that he might want to donate a lot of money, but if he did, he wasn't sure they'd agree to accept it. What would they do with it? The things they wanted most were too valuable to cost anything.

Carl Harding, who had spent a lot of time that afternoon on the filmophone, and even more hours on his own with a pen and paper, was well prepared for the meeting. He'd tried to sell projects with much bigger budgets to famous names with awards on their mantelpieces, but this one had started to matter. Like his daughter, he could be tenacious, and hard to resist.

Dave, meanwhile, had been too busy all day to collect his thoughts with any success. He was much less ready, especially as he'd been called over to the Fielders' new home an hour before the supper began, to help out with a quick bit of carpentry which didn't earn him many thanks. Ken Fielder was dour to say the least, and the boy...well, Millie would say he was troubled, but Dave would be inclined to leave off the d.

So even as Dave wandered with Millie over to the school hall, he was still trying to sort out his feelings about Carl's proposal.

Yes, he was probably a bit jealous. He didn't like his swankiness, his money, suits or famous contacts. Most of all he didn't like the way he talked to Millie, the way he smiled at her. But he knew it meant nothing. He was a smoothie, that was all, a charmer who couldn't help himself. He represented a lot of things Dave hated about New Britain, but it would be unfair to blame him personally for that. Perhaps, he told himself, this documentary could do no harm. After all, none of them would ever see it.

At the school, everyone voted, for reasons Carl could not fathom, to open up the doors and spill outside. He had been lent a thick, not very stylish kind of anorak, but chose, for the moment, to shiver a little. After a warm welcome had been extended to the newcomers, and fruit punch had been poured, he stood to address the group even before supper began.

"My daughter, my friend and I would like to thank you all for the way you have overcome the reservations that some of you felt when we made our rather flashy entrance a few days ago. You have fed us, looked after us and never allowed us to feel uninvited."

An uncomfortable Dave faced down into his punch, looking up again to see Carl smiling gratefully at Millie.

"I think you know that it was not my choice to come."

He grinned at Lia, who grinned too.

"I had ill-informed prejudices, in spite of the friendship which many of you showed me when Lia here was a baby. I was loath to leave my air-conditioned, scented home with all its creature comforts at the flick of a fingertip. But my daughter is made of stronger and more heroic stuff. Thanks to her I have seen for myself the way you support and value one another, protect and care for the planet in a way that mainland families cannot imagine – and live a dream. And it's moved me. I thank you."

Dave wondered whether this was a script like the one he'd offered them the chance to approve. It went down well, very well, and many gathered around him to wish him all the best in his consuming, polluting, chilled and plugged-in life, as the food was served. Then when everyone had eaten, he stood up to begin again, and the chatter soon faded into expectant silence.

"We are sad to leave, my daughter and I, but we have some beautiful memories to take away. I don't know how we'll begin to convey to anyone what this community is like, the how and why of it all." He directed the smile like a searchlight.

"The fact is that when I tell my neighbours, colleagues and friends about Rainbow Dreams, they will look at me blankly, because only one in a million knows about this special community, separated from the mainland by more than sea. And you may be thinking that this is exactly the way you want it to be."

Glances and murmurs confirmed that he could be right.

"But because I understand the minds and hearts of people outside, I know how attracted to your world many people would be. Okay, so they are shut down, kept away from the real things that you cherish: the earth, the sea, the living world and the spiritual dimension that underpins everything you are. But I am hoping you will let them glimpse all this, give them the chance to respond, to question themselves and their values."

He left the pause to gather weight.

"Maybe, just maybe, it just might open eyes…and souls."

Dave could stand it no longer. He found himself on his feet.

"He wants to film us. He wants to let the world in. And the question is, is it worth the risk? What are the chances that a little documentary can help us change the world before it changes us?"

"Yes, Dave, you're right. I am asking you to agree to a documentary about Rainbow Dreams, and not so little, either." He smiled. "It's just a matter of giving people a chance to witness, as we have, without eating you out of house and home – as we have."

Laughter rippled quietly across the room.

"And my promise to you is that we will not trespass, or overstay our welcome, and we will do the whole thing on a shoestring in order to ensure minimum disruption – just a presenter, a cameraman, a sound man…and me."

Dave thought the last word sounded capitalised.

"No heliplane, because we'll come by boat. No damage, and a substantial fee for you to share. And then we'll go away, and leave the island just as we found it. But we will have sown some seeds, and raised some questions that need to be asked. And I believe that's worth doing. Don't you?"

He let the silence gather.

"Do you?"

Dave felt winded and defeated. He told himself he should have paid more attention to the movies if he was going to play his part in a scene like this. Carl had anticipated all the questions, and built the answers into the pitch before anyone could ask them. And he had helped him do it.

Maybe they saw something he didn't, and not the other way round. It would not be the first time he had knotted himself up for no good reason. He made his excuses in the form of a stomach upset in order to leave early. And it was barely a lie. He felt a sickness of a kind.

"Oh," said Millie, "it must be the same thing Indira's got. Do you want me to come too?"

"No, no," he told her. "I'll be fine. You stay."

Dave knew it wasn't like him, and he was cross with himself. For the moment he was out of step with the rest, but he was sure no decision would be made in a rush.

At the school the food was being cleared and Sam was stacking chairs with help from Lia. He felt tired and wrong-footed, somehow, but stirred, because this way, it might not be over after all.

"Will you come too, to make the film?"

"If I have anything to do with it."

Sam thought it sounded quite exciting. And as no one on the island would have any way of watching the documentary when it was broadcast in homes across the mainland, Carl was offering to ship them all over to the nearest movie theatre in Greatport, to see it on a big surroundoscreen, as a kind of special preview.

At the sink, Millie knew Dave was not at all happy, but didn't understand why. She trusted Carl Harding. He was a sweet talker, of course, but she believed he was sympathetic to their ideals, and a decent man. She had seen how much he loved his daughter, so much that he would leave his work, and his home, and fly out at great expense to save the life of a sick horse just because she asked him to. She was sure he would do nothing that could threaten their relationship. And it was obvious to everyone that Lia loved the island with a passion.

Millie thought it was quite exciting too. And by the time the heliplane landed, around eleven, most of the brothers and sisters felt very much the same. It was no more than a matter of minutes between the news that the silver machine had arrived and its departure, watched by a small, waving crowd.

Among them at the front, closest to the suction and spin, Sam waved too, but his glimpse of Lia at a tiny window was brief and shaky. Almost the last thing she had done before climbing in was tell Sam that Carl had been given his answer. He could make his film. Then she had hugged him and left him, saying, "See you soon," and, a totally unnecessary, "Write to me."

Sam watched the plane lift off into darkness, a spectacularly multi-coloured light display that in mere seconds became no bigger than a star. In the absence of Dave, he claimed his mother's arm and they ambled back home.

Thirteen

October 26th 2058

Dear Sam,

Nearly a month since we left the island. How is Shadow? If he's poorly again, don't tell me. Not because I don't want to have to persuade Dad to set off on another mercy mission but because I couldn't bear it if it was all for nothing. Not that it could be, because we had such a brilliant time. Well, especially me. Dad has persuaded his favourite presenter to front the film. You won't have heard of her but of course she's absolutely stunning. You have to be stunning to front programmes. Dad says some of the presenters he's worked with are thick as two short planks but in Jenna's case, she's very bright and even knows a bit about alternative lifestyles. Did you know that's what you're living?

I keep trying to chip away at him and Mum about letting me come. The trouble is it could take more than a few days and I couldn't possibly survive if I missed so much school. My messagetape would overheat and combust with important data to pass on! As it was, the system didn't like it much that I missed a day and a half. One of my messages complained that I'd put on weight! I blame your mum for that. Academically they graded me Es for those sessions. Or rather, it did. It doesn't understand about friendship and emergencies and sick horses. Mum says I'll have to work hard to up my achievement level for the term. She's got no idea! I can hardly do anything else but work – unless I shut down my system. If only I knew how to do that secretly, I could sit quietly and read Jane Austen all day. Only of course I'd be caught on camera.

If only....!

How's Beaky? She could have been a Jane Austen character. A nice aunt. She would have put Mr Darcy straight at the first ball, and saved all that misunderstanding! It's a pity she missed the supper on the last night. How is Dave? Did he really have a tummy upset or was he in a strop? Do you think he loves your mum? I'm not sure she loves him.

Lia crossed out the last two sentences just in case. What did she know?

How have the Fielders settled in? When is their trial period over? What happens if you all decide they're not fitting in? How would you tell them? Shouldn't you let them stay anyway? If we had neighbours we didn't like we'd have to put up with them, and you're supposed to be a freer society. Anyway, that's my opinion, even though you didn't ask for it. And before you think anything, it has nothing to do with the fact that Rory is gorgeous!

I'm in a funny mood. It's partly being here when I'd rather be with you. I'd rather be on the island than anywhere, and I'd rather be anywhere than back at my beloved Grade One linegraded academy. Girls my age aren't supposed to be awkward and moody nowadays, like teenagers have always been, because of the program of hormones and chill therapy that starts at thirteen. So soon I'll be serene, whether I want to be or not. It makes me want to smash something, honestly, Sam.

I keep nagging Dad for a date to start filming. It'll have to be soon, or they'll put it off because of winter weather. We're all wimps on the mainland. Mum sends her love to your mum. Do you think they could be friends again?

Can you believe it? The shops are playing Christmas songs twenty-four seven already. It seems silly that we have to call it Winterval when we're force-fed a pan pipes version of So Here It Is Merry Christmas! There are laws now about flashing Santas and snowmen wasting electricity (and annoying people like me) but last year when some plonker got fined for his Rudolf, sleigh and elves he became a national hero! There was lots of talk about freedom, which made me mad. People have always felt free to destroy the earth. Did you know Nativity plays are banned in schools now?

Bah! Humbug! (None of my friends have heard of Scrooge.) Give Shadow a kiss from me.

Lia

Dear Millie,

I'm slipping this note in with Lia's letter because I want to thank you for looking after the two of them so generously when they visited – even though Lia invited herself! She's a strong-willed girl but she has a big heart. She thinks the world of Sam. You must be very proud of him. She also thinks you are wonderful, and I don't think Carl would disagree! When they speak of you I feel sad that I was careless with our friendship. My memories of the hospital and of Sam's naming ceremony are so vivid and happy.

I know Lia wants to be a part of the film crew but we agree she can't miss any more of her education, and Charlie missed her dreadfully last time. I would have loved to come myself. Perhaps one day.

Carl promises me the disruption during filming will be minimal. He is grateful that you have all agreed and is committed to doing a great job that you will approve.

All the very best,
Roz Harding

It's years since I wrote a letter!

By the time the two letters reached Sam and Millie it was November, and several degrees colder on the island than in mild, foggy London. Looking up at the steely sky, where dark clouds scudded quickly thanks to a bitter wind, Sam didn't rate the chances of the film crew arriving before Christmas – which the islanders flatly refused to rename Winterval.

And maybe that would be just as well. In answer to Lia's question about the Fielders, they hadn't fitted in very well at all, especially the gorgeous but rather aggressive Rory. He probably made the best argument for force-chilling that the Department of Linegraded Education could hope to find.

Not that Rory's own idea of self-medication was quite in line with expert opinion. His pharma-counsellors would have been disappointed, if not surprised, to see him at that moment, alone on the beach, scrabbling around for a rock of optimum size and hitting his head with it, harder each time, until a trickle of blood broke from his flesh to be wiped with his forefinger and licked away with his tongue.

"Sorry, Carrot Top," he said, hurling the rock into the next gathering wave. "Got the wrong boy."

In his bedroom later that evening, Sam was concealing the evidence of the mistake under his pyjama top. He rolled up the sleeve to look at the bruise that swelled purple, black and heavy between his elbow and shoulder. It was sore to the kind of careless contact that had made him wince a dozen times since Rory Fielder made a missile of a convenient stone and aimed it at him.

"With hair like that you've got to expect to be a target," he'd told him with a smile.

That was after he spat at him in the corridor. He had kicked him, too, during football but when the ball was nowhere near and neither was Dave. It was no big deal. Well, the stone wasn't that small, and the bruise was bigger. But Sam had never rated injuries, not the kind that only hurt the body. He hadn't mentioned any of it at home. Dave was nearly always there and Dave was Mr Jameson too. Not his dad. And the person he would most like to talk to was hundreds of miles away, quite possibly dreaming of somebody tall, skinny and beautiful, with hair almost as fabulous as hers.

Fourteen

When Sam knocked on the Fielders' front door the following morning, it was a courtesy. RD families never locked their doors, and tended to leave them wide open at the most tentative of sunbursts.

"Yes?" Rory's mother wanted to know.

"Hullo, Mrs Fielder. I thought I'd call for Rory – so we could walk to school."

He hadn't really thought it through. He just knew he had to stop it, and that meant confronting it. All his life Sam had heard about how fearless he was, as a little boy. He supposed he was trusting that fearlessness was something you didn't outgrow.

"How sweet!" she said, and looked amused.

She called upstairs. The hall was still full of labelled boxes, but he knew they'd turned down all the many offers of help.

"Rory! There's a friend come to play."

Rory took his time, but when he did shuffle down the stairs, he didn't quite hide his surprise. He swore at the boxes in his way but his mother took no notice.

"How are you doing, Rory?" Sam asked brightly.

"What's it to you?"

Rory was half-asleep. He didn't like mornings. And he didn't like this boy with the red hair either. He got under his skin, like an itch, and it made Rory want to scratch him.

"Don't be so rude, Rory," said his mother, and disappeared into the kitchen.

Rory gave him a stare. Sam could see he still hadn't got over his surprise that he was there. He didn't seem to know what to say for a while, but that soon changed.

"How'd you get the name Pulse? It's not like you've got your finger on any pulse, because you're out of it," he grinned, warming to his subject. "A pulse is a rhythm. And you guys haven't got any. Talk about slow. I wouldn't call you Pulse. I'd call you Coma."

Sam winced, but hoped it didn't show. This hostile boy had no right to use the name that had been so personal between him and his father. As for the rest, which he had to admit was pretty sharp, he didn't care. Water off a duck's back.

Rory was laughing, but felt its lack of sound. He wished he could remember how to do it properly. But didn't you need role models for that kind of thing?

He brushed past Sam and out of the door. Keeping his gasp of pain firmly inside, Sam followed and caught him just as he passed a couple of starlings drinking from a puddle.

"Did you think I might give them a kick?" Rory wondered, turning with a smile, thinking what a fraud he was, and how he used to feed ducks in the park in the days when you were allowed to wander free, before masks. "Or stone them, maybe," he carried on, aware of their colours, "even though they're not crows?"

"You kicked me," Sam reminded him.

"Oh...so I did. I had a go at stoning too, I seem to remember."

Sam thought he didn't sound sorry. In fact Rory wished he hadn't bothered. He'd been half-hearted – objective unclear – and it had looked as if his aim was rubbish when he could have hit him if he'd wanted to.

"Is your bruise as big as mine?" he asked Sam suddenly, lifting the hair that fell across his forehead, and grinning again, because he knew it was magnificent, in the colour and the seeping, swelling area of it. "All my own work. A true artist."

Sam wasn't sure how to arrange his face. Rory's had changed in the space of a moment, the hair curtaining the bruise and the eyes averted.

"Is it because you didn't want to come here?" Sam suggested, making sure that if he couldn't walk behind the older boy, he kept alongside him, not in front.

"Maybe it's you I don't like, not Rainbow La La Hippy Dippy Dreamland."

"You're obviously a big fan of our little community. That's good. So you're settling in well, then," said Sam, brightly.

Rory snorted and kicked his bag hard.

"What is it you don't like," Sam continued, "about Rainbow La La Hippy Dippy Dreams? Good name, by the way. Snappy."

Rory narrowed his eyes at him but his mouth was trying to grin. He reached down and pointed out the horse dung steaming in the mud. For a moment Sam thought he was going to scoop it up and hurl it at him, or smear it over one of them. In fact Rory was wondering how he could work it into a song.

"Exhibit one: crap. Two is the weather," he said, pointing up to the slate grey sky and around him at the dampness that hung cold everywhere, "which is …crap."

Sam thought he was getting his drift, but had no chance to say so. Rory was enjoying himself.

"Three is the school, where there are now two old computers in each class, probably donated by OAPs who wanted something cooler…which are total…crap. Four is the night life, which doesn't even exist. And five is the way people here think they're wise and pure when they're just a hundred years behind."

He grinned at a tuft of grass as he kicked it.

"It's such crap."

"Okay," said Sam, "I'll give you the computers. Well, I would, but you'd chuck them back. And we do have animals that don't seem to want to use a toilet, poor backward creatures. I apologise on their behalf."

Sam paused to enjoy Rory's silent reaction, but he hadn't finished yet.

"Night life at this time of year is about talking, till you're too cold to stay up, and then it's all about sleeping. But then I quite like exercising my brain instead of shutting it down in front of a screen. And I love my bed. Don't you? The other stuff is why we're here. You must be used to community life and lala hippy thinking. Was it so different in Norwich?"

Rory, who had been striding ahead and kicking stones during Sam's speech, hadn't managed not to hear, but didn't feel inclined to answer.

"Are we dippier or something?" wondered Sam. "Even more la la?"

At that Rory couldn't help grinning, very briefly.

"Well, *you* are."

Sam grinned too, just faintly.

"You'll get used to us. People here are okay, you know. They care about each other. They try to help."

"How does a wet wuss like you come to know a hot babe like Lia? I could care about her alright."

Sam's grin faded. It wasn't his fearlessness that deserted him, but his certainty, his control of what was inside him.

"That's not your business."

"Says the little boy who knocked on my door, butted in on my morning and tried to play the shrink!"

Sam could see Rory's delight at hitting a nerve.

"Don't worry," Sam told him, casually, "I can leave you alone... if you've got more friends than you need."

"Yeah. But can I leave you alone, that's the question?"

Sam didn't know how he'd thrown away the advantage when he had it, or how to get it back. And he didn't understand how anyone could let a smile drop, in an instant, into a sneer that looked like a clenched fist might come with it.

"Well, you won't kick the la la out of me," he told him, quietly, and managed a smile.

"No, I don't suppose I could. You're too far gone."

"Lia is kind of my best friend. We were born together...same hospital, same...well, same minute, nearly. We write letters. She's not my girlfriend – but I do know she's really beautiful."

"That's the first thing you've said that hasn't been...

"Crap? I could lend you a dictionary if you want to widen your vocabulary."

They had arrived at the school. Rory nodded towards it.

"My last school was linegraded. I didn't feel...like this. I was well chilled. I didn't make any trouble, not much. I sat at my station and did what I was supposed to do – most of the time.

Plenty of behaviour counselling, and medication when I needed it. I did okay. I'm not thick."

"Didn't you feel like a robot? Like they'd taken your…"

Sam held back the word soul.

"My personality? Yeah. But that's just what I liked about it."

Sam couldn't help the stare of incomprehension.

"You're the shrink," added Rory. "Work it out. Then tell my mother."

Sam waved to Robbo, noticing that he looked a bit shocked to see him walk across the playground with Rory, who swung from the beam on the apparatus and pushed the swing hard.

A five-year-old nearby ran away, and held Miss Lane's hand as she stood in the doorway to let the youngest class in. She watched Rory hard for a moment, then shut the door.

"Does Jameson live with you?" asked Rory, seeing Dave through the window, writing on the whiteboard.

"Not really."

"Is he sleeping with your mum?" But Rory put his own hand over his mouth. "Oops! Me and my big mouth!"

"Not your business," said Sam, "or mine. But Dave's okay. He's one of the good guys. Give him a chance…you know, to get to like you."

"Have you got to like me, then?"

"More than I did."

Rory hurried off, whooping a deeply ironic, overacted "Yippee!"

Sam headed towards Beaky, who was also watching at her door.

"Morning, Mrs Bird."

"Everything alright, Sam?"

"Yes, thanks, fine."

He wiped his muddy trainers on the mat in the doorway and shrugged off his coat. Time would tell.

"Morning, Rory," said Dave in the adjacent room.

"What's the story, morning glory?" just came back.

"Oasis. End of the century?"

Rory didn't give old people credit for claiming they used to be young, or for knowing music that was edgy once. He could show him edgy here and now, if he wanted. But old Jameson had that look of *adult trying to bond*, and Rory felt it would be kinder to show him straight away, before he got any ideas, that it wasn't going to happen.

"Crap," he said. "My dad sings along till you want to strangle him. Or yourself."

Rory didn't like the way Dave Jameson smiled, as if he had a preferred option. Rory was getting soft. He'd let that Sam kid off lightly. And now he was letting old lefties get one over. It was the island. La La Land was making him mushy.

That same morning, Lia went downstairs for breakfast to find her father gulping down the last dregs of coffee as he stood in his pale blue suit ready to leave for the studio.

"Ah, Lia!" he greeted her, giving her a kiss on the forehead when she hugged him. "Do you want the good news or the bad news?"

"Is the good news that I don't have to go to school?"

"No," he said wearily, "but you will be interested. We leave on Tuesday, to start filming on the island. When I say we…"

"You don't mean me."

"No. It's… well, it's not where you belong, honey. It's not real life."

"Oh, so they're playing out there? Pretending?" she protested. "Dad!"

"In a way. It's an escape, after all. Surely you can see that? It's opting out of the stuff the rest of us have to deal with. And that's maybe not so brave after all."

"So you don't want me joining in their silly games? I can't believe you, Dad! I don't know why you're making this film if that's what you think! Some hope of a balanced viewpoint! I think somebody had better warn them now so they can pull out before it's too late!"

Roz came in, flushed and flustered, hairbrush in hand, a lot less ready for Charlie than Carl was for work. It stressed her when they clashed, her husband and her independent-minded daughter.

"I hate him, Mum!"

"No you don't, Lia," her mother told her quietly, putting an arm round her. "Come on, sweetheart, chill! Have some breakfast and tell me calmly."

She turned to Carl, who looked anything but chilled himself, but picked up his briefcase and lunchbox-sized mini personal computer, kissed her cheek and turned back to his daughter. His little drama queen, he called her at work, with sighs of pride.

"Look, Lia, you've got a blind spot where Sam and his RD friends are concerned. We can talk about it later. But you've got to trust me, like they do, to be fair."

She turned away, unavailable for kissing goodbye.

"They trust you because they believed your pitch! So did I!"

"You know your father will be open-minded and objective," murmured Roz, trying to lower the volume, not least because Charlie was still asleep upstairs.

"Do I?!"

"If you really have no faith in me," said Carl, "then there's no more I can say, not now. I'll be late tonight, but I'll talk to you then, when you're more rational."

"Yeah, you'd better call the school and get them to schedule in some tablets. Or maybe an injection this time," she yelled after him as the door closed behind him.

Roz took a long, deep sigh.

"I'm okay, Mum. I'll have some breakfast; I'll get ready for school. I'll shut down and forget it."

Roz gave her daughter a questioning look as she opened a sealopak of steaming porridge from the hotbox. It didn't taste like Millie's but it was as instant as opening a door.

"I love you, Lia," her mother told her. "Don't say you hate him because I love him too."

"I know," Lia muttered. "I didn't mean it. But he treats me like a child with no…. sense.."

Before her mum could argue, she reminded her that they would both, she and Sam, be teenagers soon.

"He's not your brother, Lia," Roz told her. "You talk like you're twins. He's a lovely boy by all accounts, but you've only met him a few times in your life, and yet you seem to put him, and everything he says and does, above…everything. That's why your father said those things. It's hard for him."

Lia couldn't help feeling that in fact her father found everything remarkably easy. Including letting his daughter down.

"And he's making the film, partly, to please you, to make you happy, to show you he values what you value. Don't knock him back. He adores you. He loves you because you are yourself, in spite of everything. Can't you see that?"

Lia was silent over her porridge, until a deep and bouncy announcement, loosely translated as Ready To Play, broke out upstairs.

She looked up to her mother. Charlie would be standing in his cot trying to turn the quilt into a trampoline and looking around for company.

"Talking of brothers…!" said Lia, and ran upstairs two steps at a time to say hullo.

Roz stayed with her coffee, wondering whether there would be any point at all in taking Lia for teen chill therapy when she hit thirteen. Roz would find it easier, as her mother, if part of her didn't agree at times that she was right.

"Mum!" called Lia. "Do I really have to do the nappy? It's a corker!"

Roz grinned wearily to herself and put down her mug, remembering with a smile that Lia was once a doddle too.

Fifteen

Carl's message, sent to the island's only ae mail account address in the school office, caused a flutter of anticipation among some, but not all, of the staff in the school.

"I shan't tidy a single shelf," said Beaky. "They'll have to take us as they find us."

"Should we lock Rory Fielder in the toilets?" suggested Kara.

"He's been more settled recently," commented Dave.

Carl's message had conveyed a hi from Lia at the end, but Sam, who heard at the end of the school day, would have felt more enthusiastic about the news if she had been able to persuade her father to bring her along.

Millie hurried out at once to the garden with a trowel, prompting Sam to ask whether she was going to neaten up the herbs and check that the vegetables all looked as tidy as possible.

"Well, I can't do a lot about my hair!" she pointed out.

"If you like I could pick out the weeds and spiders' webs," Sam offered. "And then I'll do the garden too."

He would have had to shake the earth out of his own hair if his mother hadn't missed with the handful she grabbed.

Some of Sam's mates were growing hyper as the filming became imminent. Robbo decided it would be his chance to score a great goal that might impress the manager of Manchester United if he happened to be a fan of late night documentaries.

Henry began his own script, which he would ask Carl to look at, wondering whether he might get a mention in the credits.

Rory wished he hadn't had to sell his keyboard when the family moved. With it he could have played one of his own compositions and offered it as a kind of soundtrack. He couldn't imagine, though, who would want to watch a documentary about oddball dropouts. He made a mental note to tell that flash director guy about Hippy Dippy La La Land in case the programme was still in need of a title.

Indira Bird had low expectations of Carl Harding's documentary. It was surely bound to trivialise something he couldn't possibly understand. Had she not been feeling so poorly that night, she would have opposed it at the meeting. But now, as she stirred her lentil soup for one and guessed what Tom would have said about it all, she realised it was too late to do anything except refuse to get caught up in any excitement.

"Just a few days, Dave," said Millie, passing him a generous helping of vegetable chilli, "and it'll all be over."

He looked at the plateful as if it might kill him.

"Is it that bad? You didn't leave Sam in charge of it, did you?"

Sam pulled a face, but he couldn't really mind when his mum was laughing. She flicked a tea towel at Dave's back, telling him she'd thank him not to insult the cooks. Remembering Rory's questions, he told himself that if this was the way things were, then they really were together, and he'd better get used to it.

In a rather tidier home, Carl snoozed on his cream leather sofa, stretched out his legs and yawned before turning off the documentary about the history of man and the whale. It was a story that had ended in extinction. Just as well Lia was in bed, he thought.

She was such a reactive, emotional girl, so desperate to right the world's wrongs, and so sure what they were. Just like he had been. How could he explain to her that he'd meant what he said about escape – but no more than he'd meant the speech he made on the night of that supper? How could he convey to her that for someone who had lost almost everything, and worked hard all his life to get it back, it wasn't easy to deal with people who chose to throw it all away?

When, a few days later, Carl said goodbye, Charlie was fast asleep, which saved on the washing. Roz cried unexpectedly, and Lia hugged him so long and hard she must have been trying to tell him something.

"Give this to Sam, Dad, please," she said, as they separated, producing a tiny filmophone.

"It's my old one," said Roz. "She wants to be able to call him."

"She can call me."

"I know! We will. Please, Dad."

"I suppose it'll save him having to break in to his teacher's house to steal one."

"Dad!"

"Okay, okay. If it means you forgive me."

"Of course I do!"

"You're supposed to say there's nothing to forgive."

"Only everything," she smiled, and hugged him again. "Do a brilliant job, won't you? Will it be smells and all?"

"I think it should be, don't you? But a warning will go out about the advisability of shutting that function down."

"Life isn't always scented and disinfected," sniffed Lia. "Especially with this one around!" she cried, picking up Charlie, who laughed because he saw she wanted him to.

"Not again!" groaned Roz, sniffing his padded bottom.

"How could Rainbow Dreams possibly be worse than that?" cried Lia, triumphantly.

Carl was to meet the others at the station, where they would catch a long-distance high-speed monorail travelpod to the coast. There they would find a fast, state-of-the-art leisure cruiser to take them across to the island. No eyes, no masks. Just disinfected air all the way. The whole journey would take at least five times as long as the heliplane flight, but a promise was a promise. Carl had made a few of those lately.

He'd promised Jenna Dukakis five star accommodation, because that was what she insisted on. Well, Millie was a hell of a hostess.

He'd promised the guys that the island had a great little pub. But then the home-made beer was pretty good stuff, if you liked that kind of thing.

And he had promised himself that he would make more effort to get on with Dave Jameson, which might have to involve paying Millie rather less attention. Whether he'd keep the promise concerning the phone for Sam, he wasn't sure yet. These things were easily lost.

But at the end of the journey, when the team of five arrived carrying the lightest equipment current technology could provide, and a crowd of islanders gathered to welcome them at the jetty, he had hardly climbed out of the boat and onto the pebbles when he heard and felt the rhythm of an African drumbeat throbbing against the top of his thigh.

Even then it might not have been too late to turn it off and let the phone slip into the sea, but the boy was standing there, eyes on him, almost as if he knew.

He handed it over.

"For you, I think," he said.

As Sam scuttled off, Jenna slipped her arm through his. Still looking fabulous even after a wind-blown crossing and a few drinks, she whispered in his ear that she couldn't wait for a shower and a cocktail at the five star hotel.

"Look, Carl," she added, before he could reply, "let's get it straight, shall we? I get paid a ridiculous fee because I'm very, very pretty. But it doesn't mean that I'm also very, very dim."

She withdrew her arm and teetered onto the pebbles. The cameraman chuckled to himself. He had worked with Carl before, and found him easy – both to like and to mock.

"See?" he told the sound man. "Told you Carl Harding had a way with the ladies."

But the smile was wiped from his face as he stepped in the twilight in something Shadow had left behind.

Sixteen

Sam hadn't really appreciated everything that was involved in making a short documentary. There seemed to be a lot of preparation before they actually started filming. Garth and Beaky told Carl that they flatly refused to set anything up for the cameras, so he'd have to film things and people as they were, or not at all. No rehearsals. No lines. No compromise.

Sam rang Lia, every day – unless she rang him first – but there wasn't too much to tell. She wanted to know what Jenna looked like first thing in the morning.

"Grumpy. But I've never caught her without full make up. Do you think she sleeps in it?"

She asked about Rory, too, but he couldn't sum that situation up in one word, and held back on certain facts that would have shocked her – not to protect Rory but Lia. The truth was that Sam found Rory hard to like but somehow even more difficult to hate.

In fact, Sam knew that even his generous-minded mum did not know what to make of the family. Debs Fielder often wore the kind of smile that suggested she found a black humour in everything and everyone. She had upset his mum somehow or other, and then brought her a bottle of some expensive perfume as a way of saying sorry. Millie, who had lived most of her life with the free scent of earth and bread and apples, wasn't sure what to do with it and worried about the money, which might have fed an African family for months.

And then there was Ken Fielder. Sam had been meaning to tell Lia that the other night he had caught a glimpse of Rory's dad through a window, just before he pulled his curtains, without his hair. Or rather, with a short, Sleepyhead Guy kind of haircut, not his usual rather matted dreadlocks. But he hadn't had it all cut off because the next time he saw him, it was back again.

A puzzled Sam had mentioned it to Robbo, who now called him Syrup because apparently in old Cockney rhyming slang syrup of figs meant wig. He'd been meaning to ask Lia why a middle-aged brother would wear one. But now he'd rather avoid the subject of the entire family, especially as she needed no encouragement to take an interest in the son.

Sam knew Lia would see in his face, when he talked about Rory, that he wasn't telling the whole story. So he was working on his act for the phone, getting used to the idea of presenting the expression on his face as well as the tone in his voice. He even combed his hair before he rang her, but it still felt weird, looking at the tiny image of her and knowing she could see him, and read him, however small he was.

"Rory? He'll be okay, I suppose. Shadow is fit and flying. I'm giving him extra grooming," he told her. "I reckon he's got his sights set on being a movie star."

One evening during a call she held Charlie up to show him, and he must have grabbed the phone and tried to put it in his mouth. One minute his chubby, sticky face was filling the tiny screen and Sam could smell the honey, and the next all he could see was a rolling wave of tongue slobbering around little stumpy baby teeth, before normal service was resumed in the shape of a giggly Lia.

"Oh man, I've never been so sure that I couldn't be a dentist!" he told her. "I didn't ask for a tonsil tour!"

"I told you he'll eat anything!"

Then on day three of filming Lia picked up the filmophone to see long fingers plucking guitar strings. Someone who couldn't actually hold the phone was singing in a nasal and stylised voice which made the lyrics hard to hear.

"Out of the sky...she came...and since I met that girl nothing in my life has been the same...When she hung out at my school I felt so dumb and so uncool...like a great long-legged, wordless, no smile fool..."

At which point the little phone, which must have been propped up somehow, fell with a thud, and she saw a glimpse of bedroom floor littered with socks and scraps of paper scrawled with bad handwriting.

"Rory?"

It was a guess, but when a face appeared, looking rather sheepish, it confirmed she was right.

"Uh...you got me."

The silence was embarrassing at both ends.

"Did Sam lend you Mum's old phone? You're not supposed to throw it round the room, you know. It cost a fortune."

"Sorry. I have borrowed it, yeah, but he didn't quite lend it."

"Well give it back! He might be hunting all over for it."

"Just wanted to sing you the song I wrote. Dave Jameson lent me the guitar. I mean actually lent it. It's practically an antique. His grandad played it back when Dylan was a hip young dude."

"Oh. That's great, Rory, but…"

"But I nicked Sam's phone. Your phone. Okay, I'm gone, but don't obsess, right? I'll slip it back in his school bag. He'll never know unless you tell him."

As the screen blanked she was opening her mouth to ask him a rather delicate question about the song, but then she thought she probably knew the answer.

She didn't tell Sam, in the end. Events overtook them, in the form of the start of filming, and for her, a spot of trouble at school.

The following day was a disaster from the start, when her filmophone was confiscated by the Behaviour Police, for the third time in a row. Well, for those three days Sam had been on the other end of it. Of course she needed to be able to keep in touch! Every day she'd been even more ingenious about how to conceal the thing, but the system had more eyes than a peacock and, it turned out, lacked the decency not to scan the bra where she had lodged it.

This meant a formal sanction. Behaviour report logged. Worse, though, it also meant a lost break session, so no mid-morning sunlight through the playcentre dome.

Then the messagetape informed her that she had lost weight, and must sign on for food disorder counselling.

"What? It's only a few weeks since you were ticking me off for putting on a few pounds thanks to eating some real food! You want to make up your so-called mind," she retorted, only to find that her own particular station was miked because of her unco-operative attitude.

Behaviour warning . Yellow card flashing on screen.

She wasn't surprised to read that her study scores from the previous day left something to be desired. She wasn't in the mood anyway, but it certainly hadn't helped that she'd managed to find an old BBC adaptation of Pride and Prejudice stored in an archive she didn't even know she could access. And spent more than five hours watching it.

Somehow or other, the red lights she expected to flash up, almost as soon as the opening credits began, never butted in to spoil her pleasure, and no BP officer appeared at her shoulder. Unable to believe her luck that one of those peacock eyes was taking a bit of a techno-snooze in the form of a very welcome malfunction, she just tucked herself in and enjoyed every moment.

She might even have got away with it if she hadn't emitted a slightly swoony sound just as the system decided to mike her for her personal assessment of whether the real objective (about marketing tools) had been achieved.

Goodbye Mr Darcy.

She'd blown it now. She'd have to catch up on those unfulfilled objectives on top of the exciting new ones set out for today! Her own personal timetable appeared with graphics, music and all, dancing about on her screen as if she was supposed to squeal with glee. It promised her a hi-achievement program, with a shortened lunchtime break and without the usual daily social interaction.

"Can they do that?" she asked out loud.

SANCTIONS AS CONSEQUENCE OF INAPPROPRIATE BEHAVIOUR WERE OUTLINED IN LINEGRADED PROSPECTUS came right up on the messagetape. Instantly.

But that meant she would not speak to a real, live, flesh and bone human being all day, until her mother picked her up at seven that evening!

Fascist pigs, she thought, silently. Without a sound she declared, within her, like a chant, *I hate the system. Down down down with linegraded education. May God pull the plug ....and let it die.*

She waited, with a smile, for the hand on her shoulder, for the flashing red lights. Nothing. Punching the air in triumph, she celebrated her secret victory.

But she often wondered how long it would be before the system could read her mind. Her chill status was something she had been working on, trying to find a way of fooling it. The measurements it took were physical: heart rate, temperature, breathing pattern, visual analysis of the eyes and mouth, lie detector vibes. They only interpreted the body. She was sure there must be a way of using her mind and spirit to override and confuse, to block or distort the reading. She just hadn't found it yet.

By the time she got home that night, Charlie was already asleep and she'd missed her father calling to say that filming had begun. She was so hungry she ate most of a red label chocolate cake that her father must have bought illicitly – probably wearing a false beard and shades.

Then she turned off her phone and went to bed, wondering whether the morning messagetape would combust in confusion. It wouldn't know whether to be appalled at her massive calorie intake, or congratulate her that she'd been taken off the anorexia risk list.

Sam did try to call her, but didn't leave a message. So she didn't hear about a rather different behaviour problem in Dave's class, captured on camera in all its drama. Or Beaky's request that the incident be left out of the film, because it wasn't representative of school life on the island, and Carl's hasty assurance that he wouldn't want to show anyone in a bad light. That was definitely not what his documentary was about.

Instead, Lia slept, but badly.

In her dream, which seemed to be on a loop repeating through the night, she saw the island from the air, surrounded by thunderclouds, loud and black.

As she flew closer she saw her father, in his white suit, surrounded by a swarm of vans bouncing around in the mud. They were all jumping up and down with happy, cruel faces (even the vans), stamping hard as they landed, like bullies flattening a sandcastle. They were all trying to sink the island into the sea.

She gasped as she saw the beach at one edge of it dipping like a top-heavy inflatable into the water, and Shadow, who was galloping along it, tumbling off and whinnying in fear as the swell lifted above his head. And still they all kept jumping and cheering as Rainbow Dreams began to tilt like the Titanic and go down…down…while they jumped across to the mainland to clap and cheer as it disappeared.

Seventeen

When Carl returned home, looking worn, Lia pestered him so relentlessly for details that it left him very little mental energy for anything but a saunuzzi. But there was a report from the linegraded academy on his screens and it wasn't going away.

Roz was worried that Lia would get used to being awkward and difficult, and start to rebel in more destructive ways, that she would leave school with a poor achievement record, and that the teen chill program for which she would soon qualify would only crush her spirit.

Carl, who had been to a school where pupils were strip-searched for knives and one teenage boy once shot another, was thankful that his precious girl's Level One school for academic pupils was a safe, clean, calm place where no one was bullied or pushed teachers against the wall.

If only Lia could play the game, and come out at the other end with the spectacular achievement record that should be possible for a girl with such fierce intelligence, he believed she could do just about anything. No one had more fire. And the chill program would help, he said, by giving her the balance she lacked, by knocking off her sharp edges and helping her to be at peace with herself.

He would talk to her.

If Lia was at war with anyone or anything, Roz wasn't sure it was herself, but she didn't say so. Sometimes, when she looked at Carl, she didn't think she knew or understood him any more. She didn't see why her daughter should have to bury her spark in a school that made her unhappy, but, as she pointed out, short of going to live at Rainbow Dreams, she couldn't see any alternative.

"Well that's the heart of the problem, isn't it? I've been slow to see it, but it's clear as day now. She'll never settle here while she's daydreaming about that island, romanticising, idealising. She's in love with the whole place – fog, dung and all. And it's my fault. I shouldn't have given in over the horse and I shouldn't have made the film." He paused. "For more reasons than one."

Roz was curious because he was normally so pleased with himself when he'd just canned his footage, and so eager to start shaping it. But compared with her daughter's happiness, it didn't seem to matter, so she let the comment go.

Instead she told him she didn't agree, that it could only be good for Lia to see another way of living, that it must give her the kind of balance he himself had talked about.

She did not add that she would sooner leave her fragrant white home, climb in a boat, and go with Lia to become an RD sister, than cut her off from a world where she was truly happy.

For a while Carl kept the images in the camera, hesitating over how to finish the job. It was left to Lia to push and prompt and quiz him till he gave in and set off to the editing suite. And eventually he conceded, on returning home late a few days later, that it was done.

"Can I see it?"

"Now? What about the Comedy Hour? It starts soon."

"Oh, I'll risk another nagging tick-off on my morning messagetape. That'll make a change. Won't I get my laughter quota from Rainbow Dreaming, then?"

"I hope not! This is serious television. The BBC are interested you know, not just any old fly by night channel, but the official and the best."

He click-loaded it onto the panoramoscreen in her bedroom, kissed her on the forehead and headed for the door.

"Dad! Watch it with me."

"I've been watching it all week. I can't see or hear it any more. I don't even know if it's any good, or whether you'll be speaking to me by the time it's finished."

"Don't be stupid, Dad! It'll be brilliant. Clear off, then, if you're going, and leave me in peace."

She lay down on the bed and started it. A burst of electric guitar, like a sob wrenched from a broken heart, tore into the room, breaking up into bells, a flute and a distant piano. Lia had not been prepared for the opening shot, an aerial view closing quickly in, so much like her nightmare that she almost gasped. The minicam on the heliplane on the first trip! She'd forgotten. Even though no black cloud surrounded the island, and nobody was jumping up and down in an attempt to sink it, she felt a stab of anxiety.

Mist swirled around her walls as Rainbow Dreams woke up to a winter morning. She could almost taste the air, and chose not to censor the smells.

"On a tiny island few could name or identify on a map of Britain, there lived, in the 1970's, a community of hippies."

The words Tom Bird, horse whisperer and co-founder at the age of 19 of Rainbow Dreams Community, appeared across a black and white photo which, as the camera pulled back, was shown to be resting on Beaky's window sill, with the sun behind it. Lia hoped her dad had asked nicely to do that.

"What almost nobody on the mainland knows is that now, in this very different century, there remains a community of people of all ages living more or less exactly as Tom Bird and his friends lived then," continued Jenna.

Overlapping and repeated hand-knitted jumpers, old shapeless jeans, beards and long, neglected hair moved around the room with dogs, chickens, ducks, goats and bikes as Rainbow Dreams began to busy itself for another day. Lia couldn't help bouncing with excitement at the sight of each familiar face.

"Of the fifty-nine inhabitants of Rainbow Dreams, most are couples with children. Garth, a builder, plasterer, carpenter and general Mr Fix-it, is the son of one of the original founders and father to Christy and Kate."

"Yo, Garth!" cheered Lia as his face loomed large and rather ruddy, sawing in the workshop by the watermill.

Then Gareth was explaining that both his daughters went away to university on the mainland, but one of them, Christy, had brought Paris, the boyfriend she met on her philosophy course back to the island and was now expecting his baby.

"What? Nobody told me!" cried Lia, looking at Christy and seeing that yes, there was a bump to be smoothed round with the palm of her hand.

"All Garth's training was done on the island. In recent years he masterminded the newer cottages fitted with solar panels, light traps, warm earth heating…. and a little electricity when all else fails."

Sweeping shots of cool green features reminded her how clever RD people were, for simple-minded duffers who lived in the past.

"But not everyone was born and bred at Rainbow Dreams. Others are newcomers."

Cut to quite a flattering close-up of Kara Lane working with a group of new readers, and then sitting elegantly, long legs crossed, presumably talking to an unseen Carl.

"Well, I didn't know what to expect, exactly, but I wanted to teach, not counsel, assess or police. And I wanted to do it in the flesh, you know? It's early days, but I really don't miss many things any more."

"What do you miss?" asked her dad's voice, although the screen still offered no glimpse of him, not even the back of his head.

Kara smiled shyly, but brightly.

"Dancing in a club on a Friday night."

The camera alighted on the bow of a fiddle, and people in parkas and duffel coats either clutching mugs of steaming soup around a fire or clapping and linking arms to spin each other round. Hardly typical of Friday nights as far as Lia knew, but good when contrasted with quick shots of a dark, flash-lit, pumping West End club and young women Kara's age in tiny skirts and tinier tops, but enormous heels.

"In the community there is no pub or restaurant, although in the school there is a hall that doubles as a wet-weather meeting place"

Images from snooker table to chatting mums, to plates of flapjack slabs, toddlers and push-along toys. The aroma of coffee wafted its way towards Lia.

"There is no dentist, no vet, no lawyers, estate agent, building society or bank, no shopping mall or hairdresser."

She thought it rather mean of Dad to pick those particular heads of hair for close-ups, albeit brief and anonymous. After all, Millie was quite sharp with a pair of scissors and kept Sam's looking naturally funky.

Then the camera swept inside the surgery to the doc, father to Lars. He was using a stethoscope on Christy's belly to hear the baby's heart beating clear and strong.

"There is no ultra-sound scan or 3D holographic transformer for Christy to see her baby and be sure it's healthy," noted Jenna. "RD beliefs embrace a trust in Nature and reject gene culture and baby planning, so she and Paris will take what comes, and be thankful. The community doctor is Sven Henrikson, a holistic healer specialising in homeopathy, acupuncture, reflexology and reiki."

Ooh! Over to Ancient Geeky stretching his legs on a sofa covered in a woven throw, while Sven works on one foot. Camera to Sven's very calm, almost inanimate face.

"Since I arrived on the island in 2023," said Sven, "there have of course been deaths from old age, but apart from that, and one drowning in a storm, which was very sad..."

George McAllister! The sound of the sea, loud and angry, and just for the briefest of moments, a tang of salt in the air. Poor Sam. Poor Millie. For the first time, Lia pictured it, the broken boat, the washed up body.

"....we have had no illnesses that could not be treated here, without resort to mainland technology. Bad accidents are different – but since we have no cars, no alcohol abuse or fights, they are rare."

No thanks to Sam and his climbing on school roofs, thought Lia. Or his thirst for sea water.

"Some RD brothers and sisters are teetotal. Others brew their own beer or make their own wine," observed Jenna.

No! Not the socks! Whose were those?

"All are vegetarian, growing as much of the food they need as climate and money will allow."

"Millie!" cried Lia, fondly, as the stripy jumper bent to tend the herb garden and Lia took a deep, pleasurable breath of mint and basil. Dave was digging vigorously in the background, keeping his back to the camera which moved in on Millie's flushed and freckled face. Her dad had called her luminous and Lia reckoned the camera agreed.

"I guess we're all farmers up to a point, and our diet is probably one reason we don't have a lot of health problems," Millie said, smiling. "We let Nature dictate what's in season and try to manage without whatever she can't provide."

"Sam, where are you?" cried Lia, but as if in answer, there he was, pounding some dough in the kitchen.

"Good point about sexual equality, Dad. Nice one," she grinned to herself, hoping for a shot of one of the women sorting out the plumbing under a sink later on. Oh, bliss! Sam was getting the bread out of the oven now, no black smoke billowed out and the smell was unbelievable. He didn't foul up every time! Or was that the seventh take?

She savoured the moment.

"But the community cannot be totally self-sufficient and once a month there is a boat trip to the mainland with a list. And once a week a rather more twenty-first century boat calls to collect fruit, veg and home-baked cakes and bread to sell in the nearest town."

Humorous juxtaposition of rowing boat and loud, shiny cruiser roaring off at speed. This led into the comments of shoppers on the mainland singing the praises of the RD produce they were buying, unpackaged and additive-free. One lady also said it was a pity there wasn't a weekly tour over to the island so they could "see what goes on".

"Oh good idea!" snorted Lia. "They could set up a souvenir shop selling dreadlock wigs and T shirts saying *I've been rainbow dreaming! Have you?*"

"Not an idea that would be welcomed on the island," said Jenna, "where their separation from New Britain is seen as the secret of their physical and mental health and where the life we live is perceived as a threat, not only to the community but to the planet."

"Go Dad! Stir it up!" approved Lia as a collection of overlapping faces and voices condemned chilled and plugged-in Britain, where people, the brothers and sisters said, were poisoning the earth and their own bodies and minds.

Haunting music overlaid images: packaged food, smokers puffing away in the rain outside offices, celebrity gossip magazines, tabloid headlines, trash T.V. moments that made her turn queasily away, intersecting with melting glaciers, hurricane destruction and jammed motorway traffic. Even eyes, dull in mask holes. Lia looked away to give Blancmange a reassuring stroke, but all too understandably, she had slipped away.

"It is a non-smoking community because as Sven says, life is too precious to poison it. There is no chilling, by medication or by psycho-intervention counselling, because they believe that wellbeing springs from being at peace with the earth. And there is much more to Rainbow Dreams ideology than healthy living."

Oh dear, thought Lia. Idle curiosity satisfied, this could be where the chilled masses switched off.

"Even though," continued Jenna, "it's a tricky ideology to pin down and it does seem to depend who you talk to…"

"Dad?" cried Lia, uneasy at once. "What are you playing at?"

For the first time, Lia realised that she would not forgive him for mocking or undermining them. Meanwhile individuals on screen tried to put into words the beliefs that kept them together, but their thoughts were presented as fragments that were left incomplete.

"The whole idea of God is too big to tie down, to limit with words and package in a doctrine you have to sign up to. That's why God is God, and it's pointless trying to agree on a list of beliefs…"

Ooh, Dave! Deep stuff. Cut to a group of worshippers, eyes closed, standing still in the circle of stones, hair blowing in the wind, one or two hands raised.

"…that the spirit of Jesus is joyous, and one with other spirits that reach out with love through the Buddha or Mohammed.."

Blimey! Who was that?

"… I myself embrace classical Islam and the mysticism of the Sufi, who celebrate in dance their oneness with earth and heaven…"

Beaky, bless her! That sounded all right. Lia liked dancing, but privately. She could understand why these dancers would not perform for the camera.

"It's love, that's all. Love is what binds us. Love of one another, and the earth, and the God within us and around us, and everything pure and beautiful – like a flower, like birdsong, like art and music and poetry that stems from love – that helps us to love better," said Christy, sitting holding one hand on her bump, the other given to Paris and linked with his.

"You tell 'em, Christy!" cried Lia.

"It's simple, really," smiled Christy.

"What's wrong with that?" retorted Lia, feeling defensive now.

Jenna appeared, walking around the church of nature, agreeing that it did sound very simple, and attractively so, and picking up the petals that lay inside the ring of stones, letting them fall through her fingers, in sunlit slo-mo, before she faced the camera.

"But are the brothers and sisters at Rainbow Dreams bound by love in their daily lives? Do they really love better than the rest of us?"

But that wasn't what Christy meant, thought Lia. Come on, Dad! She wasn't comparing, boasting. She was talking about each of them trying to get closer to the way it should be, not trying to claim they were all perfect.

"On the mainland we have eliminated most of the violence from our streets and our schools. A recent study shows that 95% of us feel less stressed, less angry and afraid than we used to before integration, the chilling program and linegraded education."

There were shocking images from the first couple of decades of the century to remind those old enough to remember the days of gun crime, drunken brawling and vandalism. Then strident minor chords gave way to quiet streets, and the new estates with pan pipes floating on the scented air of their long white corridors.

"So," said Jenna, "do the hippies of this little island live up to the old ideals of love and peace?"

"Do you, Jenna?" objected Lia, the sinking feeling making it to her stomach. "Are you a saint?" She called out from the bed to the closed door. "And neither are you, Dad!"

There followed a sharp snippet from an argument between Debs Fielder and her neighbour about who had the right to pick the apples from a tree between two cottages. Debs used a language riper than the fruit until she was faded out, so that Jenna could observe that, "Not everything is shared."

From an armchair in a living room came an answer to a question about relationships, married or otherwise, as Robbo's mum supposed that if she was honest, there had, over the years, been the occasional problem between couples.

A jagged cut took the viewers back to the same face, no longer composed and objective. Yes, she herself had cheated on Robbo's dad, many years ago, with his neighbour, who had long since left the island.

"Does your husband know?" probed her dad's voice, quiet and gentle, while Hazel began to cry, hands clasped restlessly in front of her.

"Yes…and he forgave me, because...you know, he's a good man ...but I haven't really forgiven myself. And the…other person…I hurt him badly. I think he really loved me. I caused a lot of pain."

"Dad, for God's sake! Are there no affairs in New Britain? Come on!"

Lia imagined her father jumping up and comforting Hazel as the filming stopped. He would have been so kind. She could hear him assuring her that if course it would be edited out. *Naturally. No worries.* He was good at soothing.

And then her room became a classroom. Dave Jameson and his teenagers loomed large around her walls, one of them shouting and swearing at him.

Lia recognised the voice before she saw Rory Fielder, white-faced with anger. He was ranting and it wasn't musical. A tear trickled down her cheek as she watched Rory lift from across his desk an old guitar. It was the one he had used, a day or two before, to play his song about her, and the one he had apparently refused to stop playing in a geography lesson. He held it up by the neck.

"Have it back, then! I don't want your crappy old jumble sale relic! Take it, go on – and stick it!"

He was brandishing the guitar like a weapon. Dave was trying to take it and duck away from it at the same time. Then the fingers that had made it sing suddenly loosed their grip, and it crashed against a cupboard with a hollow chordless groan, knocking a pile of books thudding to the floor. A string snapped with a high-pitched protest and lay frizzing like a torn-out hair.

The camera left the abandoned guitar to pick up the shocked faces of a couple of girls and to linger a moment on Dave's expression of fazed frustration.

"Look what you made me do!" yelled Rory.

Lia thought she heard an edge to his shout where it almost tipped into a sob. But the camera didn't want to linger on a tear of vulnerability when it could have hard knuckles and splintered wood.

"The school," said Jenna, as Rory made a choice gesture to the camera before covering his face, "uses, some would say quaintly, the turn of the century National Curriculum model as a starting point. But this is interpreted by the staff of four with what Darius O'Dell, the Headmaster, calls flexibility and spontaneity. He maintains that discipline is not a problem, and insists that learning is real. Without formal assessment to show progress…."

Okay, enough. Lia knew the school didn't have graphs to prove the children were learning. The kids didn't have profiles of stacked up scores. But she didn't want to hear it. Silence filled her room and her walls stilled, returning to shiny shell-pink once more. No trace of field or apple tree, rose petals or freshly-dug earth lingered behind.

The hour of comedy therapy was beginning downstairs and she heard Carl laughing on cue. Did he care what she thought? Would he bound up any minute, hoping for her seal of approval? Or would he fall asleep, so cheered and warmed that he'd forget the tears he'd stolen and used?

She shut her room into curtained darkness at the push of a button, and lay on the bed, hugging a cushion, until Blancmange curled back in round the door and jumped up beside her. Lia stroked her, feeling her warmth and the throaty tremor of her breathing.

"I'm sorry, Sam," she told the cat. "I'm sorry. I'm sorry."

Eighteen

"Have you brought that old phone back with you?" Lia asked her father. "Or is it still there? Has Sam still got it?"

Carl looked up from his paper. It was Saturday and he was going to work late. He was surprised to see Lia standing in the doorway, her face hostile, her tone flat as she denied him so much as a hullo.

"Whoah, honey! Which question shall I answer?" He paused. "Hey, what did you think?"

"My question first," she said. "Have you brought it back?"

"Uh, yeah. Millie insisted. You don't need it, do you? I don't know where I put it. Is there a problem with your new one?"

"No, not with my phone," she said coldly. "I'm glad. I'm glad Sam can't call me, because if he did I'd have to tell him what I think of your documentary."

She saw the wave of anxiety cross his face as she spoke.

"Lia…" he began.

"Don't, Dad. I don't want to talk about it, I really don't. You've made them seem like nutters and hypocrites. And the thing is, because of the beliefs you mocked, because of the love stuff you took apart, they might forgive you. But I never will."

"I wasn't mocking anything! I told you, Lia, I was going to tell it like it is, warts and all, a balanced view. Not some kind of recruiting ad. I'm not a PR man, and I don't do fan worship. Objective is what I do. The whole picture, both sides."

"I didn't know there were sides. Love and peace, remember, Dad? Not war."

She had gone back to her room before he could ask her if she'd seen it all, right to the end. He put down the paper and was about to head up the stairs when she appeared at the top.

"Lia..."

"Catch!" she said, and chucked the film down to him.

She had thought about other places to throw it, but it would be hard, if she did, for him to edit it the way she hoped he would.

"I stand by it, Lia," he said to the silence after she had disappeared, wondering how to tell her to her face.

As he explained to Roz, when she emerged from Charlie's room, he couldn't allow such emotional blackmail.

"But I don't understand. What is it about the film that she's so upset about?" asked Roz, sitting Charlie comfortably for his breakfast.

Carl exchanged broad grins with his son, who was busy trying to grab the spoon from his mother's hands.

"Oh, I forgot the special effects," he said. "The haloes round their heads."

Fielders excluded, of course, he thought to himself. He remembered the way Debs had seemed to kick off the altercation over the apples pretty much on cue when she saw them coming, almost for the hell of it. And Ken had approached him quietly on the first night, a hidden cigarette in his hand, and asked him to make sure he didn't catch him in the corner of any shot at all. They were an odd pair, not right for the place.

As for the pretty boy, Carl reckoned chill sessions would do him the world of good, and be of benefit to the whole community, but of course people like Dave would rather have his lesson wrecked and his guitar thrown round the room than give the poor lad any medication that would crush his true and unpleasant self.

In the end, Carl took the film back to the editing suite. Hurt, he spent the day offloading onto Jenna, who told him he mustn't touch it. They watched it together, reassuring one another that it was a good, honest, even-handed piece of work.

Hadn't Lia been happy to see Sam's artwork on lingering camera, silently speaking volumes? Hadn't she enjoyed the expressions on pupils' faces during a poetry lesson, saying more about inspiration than any commentary he could write? Didn't she like the touching interview with Millie, who recalled all "the loving, practical support that had surrounded her" when her husband was drowned?

Carl couldn't understand why she was being so melodramatic about it all. Jenna was right: he should be proud of it.

So he spent some time negotiating a date for broadcast on the national schedule early in the year. Late night, of course, but he'd never expected to top the ratings. A nomination at an awards ceremony, however, would be very welcome, and might make the women of the house see things a little differently.

On the island, life for most brothers and sisters had returned to normal very quickly. Almost everything was unchanged, although Debs Fielder became less abrasive, and less possessive about apples. But Millie spent more time than usual with Hazel, Robbo's mum, who spent more time than usual crying.

She was reassured, however, by Millie's certainty that Carl would not dream of using any sensitive personal footage in the film.

"I couldn't write and ask him," she told Hazel. "He'd be so wounded that we even had to check."

For the majority, it might have seemed as if the outsiders with their fancy electronic equipment had never intruded on their life together, if it hadn't been for the large sum of money which had been divided up equally among the households. Not that any of them had much idea what to do with it.

Rory would have liked the latest surroundosound keyboard, but it would have to wait until he had escaped to the world that didn't count each kilowatt of electricity as if it were gold. He had mended his relationship with the unfortunate guitar and mumbled a sorry to Dave, who asked him to share his apology with the whole class.

"I'm an attention-seeker," he muttered, feeling like anything but.

"Cameras too much to resist?"

"Yeah. I always was a show-off. That's why I'll make it one day. When I find my own audience."

"We can find you a small but friendly one at Christmas," Dave told him, "if you're interested."

In spite of an initial snort of contempt for anyone who might make up that audience, it seemed in the end that Rory was not so much interested as desperate to take centre stage. And some of that audience clapped him pretty vigorously, which led him to consider the possibility that there might be people of taste among the sad morons that populated the island.

As Beaky had said in the remainder of the documentary, Rainbow Dreams prepared for Christmas in a way that was traditional not in the previous century but in late Victorian times, before the money-making, booze and glitter swamped it. But minus the turkey and bacon rolls. Millie and Sam both loved the creativity, the baking smells that were unique to that one time of year, the ways they found to decorate the cottages without tinsel or flashing lights.

The school followed two practices that had been in decline for a very long time until linegraded education put them out of their misery: the nativity play and the carol concert.

As Darius O'Dell had told Carl on camera towards the end of his film, "We don't pretend Christianity is the only thing that the people of the world have ever believed in. But we also don't pretend Christmas is about anything else."

Sam's letter to Lia, inside a Christmas card he'd made himself, was written after the festivities were over, but before the new BBC aired a certain documentary across the mainland.

Dear Lia,

Not much of 2058 left. It might even all be over by the time you get this. I know your Christmas isn't the way you'd like it to be. (I can't believe it's politically incorrect to call it that. Winterval is kind of clever but it sounds so grey.) But at least you're together, the four of you and Blancmange, and you can forget linegraded education for a week or so. Have you slipped through any more cracks in the system lately, or made a few of your own? Go girl!

Lia's Winterval would have been happier and less complicated if she had forgiven her father more wholeheartedly. It wasn't that she didn't want to believe his assurances about the film, that he'd worked on it, and that there was plenty of positive stuff to balance the bits for which she had hated him. She just wasn't sure she could.

She wanted to trust him as her mum begged her to, and trust that their relationship with Rainbow Dreams, her relationship, would not be broken. But in spite of the words and hugs of apology on both sides, she felt as if something else, something between the two of them, had changed. She was not his little girl any more.

You haven't said anything about the film. Have you still not seen it? It seems years since they packed up and left. Robbo would like a signed filmocard of Jenna, by the way. He was too shy to ask when she was here. But he'd kill me for telling you. He wants to know if the cameras caught his overhead kick into goal. What an exhibitionist! Dave is hoping for Rory's sake that his little tantrum with the guitar got edited out, especially as he hasn't done anything demented since. His dad is friendlier these days. Maybe they've got used to us and our nutty ways.

Shadow would send his love if he could.

He could add that Rory would do the same if he gave him a chance. Instead he asked what she was doing for her birthday, said he wished they could spend it together, thought about crossing that bit out, but left it. It was true. He did. Then he signed it and slipped it inside the card.

Garth and Beaky had both been asking him if he had heard from Lia, and he'd made out that the month of silence was not unusual, but he didn't understand why she hadn't written. And he knew that some of the brothers and sisters were equally puzzled by the lack of news from that handsome and charming film director, who had shaken their hands and promised to be in touch very soon.

Was there something she wasn't telling him?

By the time it reached her, Winterval had segued into New Year. Folding the letter and adding it to the others in her box, Lia grabbed her phone. She wasn't supposed to call her father at work, but this was an emergency.

"Rainbow Dreaming, BBC5 10:45 Friday," she read from the T.V. schedule on her laptop as soon as he picked up and appeared on her little screen, a slightly grumpy question on his face. She transferred it to her laptop so she could get a closer look at his eyes.

"Yes? So? Lia, I'm busy, honey."

"You haven't invited them to see it first like you promised. Transport laid on, remember? Panoramoscreen and sugar-free popcorn? The chance to vet it, you said."

"Look, Lia, you're really going to have to leave this to me."

"But you haven't done anything. And people across New Britain are going to be watching it at the end of the week."

"Not many people."

"That's not the point, Dad. You owe it to them."

"Of course, sweetheart. Leave it to me. I'll see you tonight."

Technology, for all its spellbinding brilliance, would never be one hundred percent reliable. Carl's ae mail to the school office fell through some sort of hole which was never identified and which he could only put down to glitches, gremlins or the seriously outdated computer system they made do with over there.

When Rainbow Dreaming was aired late that Friday night in January, only days before Sam and Lia turned thirteen, nobody on the island had seen it, or received the invitation to do so.

The reviews were so encouraging that Jenna sent him a bottle of champagne, but they'd been right about the viewing figures. The general public showed a limited interest in the lifestyle of a handful of hippies on some remote island – but there were relatives of RD families who made a point of watching, but wished they had missed it.

In York, a computer troubleshooter called Matt had tuned in out of nostalgic curiosity. He had once had another life as part of the community, but left suddenly when he could no longer bear to live next-door to the young, married woman he loved. Matt had worked hard at forgetting Hazel, and tried not to think of her as the love of his life. He was unprepared, as he sat down with his cocoa, for her tears or his own.

The senior MI5 operative who had sent Ken Fielder undercover to the island was satisfied. The filming had been awkward timing, a complication. But at least the documentary provided valuable information, which was more than their agent seemed able to do.

Ken himself might be a liability, but clearly these harmless oddballs represented no security threat of any kind. No one was growing illegal drugs to sell on the mainland. No one was making primitive bombs to reduce key cities to ashes – out of which new rainbow dreaming communities might grow. They were in fact doing nothing to undermine the fabric of society in New Britain, and could be left to carry on opting out unless the public demanded otherwise. And on the whole, the public seemed dozily indifferent.

But in a different government building, *Rainbow Dreaming: a documentary by Carl Harding* was debated in meetings at the highest level. For not many miles from the Chill

Centre where Lia waited silently for her first special teen therapy, bureaucratic wheels were being set in motion at the Department of Linegraded Education.

Nineteen

January 17th 2059

Dear Sam,

Thirteen at last! Thanks for the gorgeous birthday present. I'm wearing it now. You don't know how talented you are! Really, Sam! The drawing looks just like me, only prettier. It's so clever the way you've drawn my eyes. I didn't know what to send you. I know the chocolate candle is a naff gift for people who have everything else, but you can save some electricity and drink in the aroma at the same time. Luckily Charlie isn't there to try to eat it.

I'm sorry I didn't write. I've been too chilled to get off the couch! Joke. You'd have to ask my parents whether the hormone treatment and counselling are a good investment of government money. I haven't thrown anything at my dad lately. People are so frightened of anger. Wasn't Martin Luther King angry at racial inequality? Wasn't Gandhi angry that the British were running India? It doesn't mean you want to beat up anyone or blow up anything. But there are things we should be angry about and I don't intend to give up.

That brings me to the film. I've been very angry with my dad. I did know before you did, and I should have told you. I felt like he'd betrayed you – and me – but I was told I was being emotional and unreasonable and must trust him. I know he didn't mean to stir up any trouble and I know he thought he was doing a good job. Mum says I don't understand – and she's right, I don't. He says it was all a mix-up that you never got the

159

invitation to the special showing, and blames the old computer in the school office. He's tried to get in touch with Garth and Beaky to try to explain. I don't know what to say. Maybe it was fair. Maybe it was unfair. But I wish it was never made.

Please don't blame him any more than I do. Write back soon.
Lia

P.S. His next project may be a profile of Harder to Fall. Is it mean of me to suspect that he's trying to bribe me into forgiving him when he talks about arranging for me to meet them in the recording studio?

February 15th 2059
Dear Lia,

Thanks for the candle. Mum loves to come for a sniff when I'm burning it. I'm glad you're wearing the pendant.

Don't let them change you. Don't let them shut down your emotions. It's so wrong. I wish they would just leave you alone to be you.

I knew about the film. People on the mainland who knew people here told them about it one way or another. Some people are a bit upset but then it's a sensitive thing, the way people see you, isn't it? They'll get over it. Mum is worried about Hazel (that's Robbo's mum) for some reason. She must have been on the film and apparently she just keeps crying. Robbo doesn't know what's wrong with her.

Anyway it isn't your fault. Nobody hates your dad either, even Dave, who is upset to hear that he kept Rory in the film. We just want to get on with things.

Sam

He hadn't told her the whole truth and he felt bad about that, but then she hadn't told him everything either and he understood why.

He hadn't told her that a man called Matt, who used to live on the island, had arrived out of the blue, made Robbo's mum cry even more, been asked to leave, and politely refused.

He hadn't mentioned that Rory had told him his family might be leaving too. Or that Darius O'Dell had apparently told Dave, who'd told Millie, that there was a sudden flurry of ae mails from the Department of Linegraded Education asking a lot of unanswerable questions.

He couldn't tell her, because he didn't know, that Garth and Faye, and Beaky too, were sending back their share of the money, but he knew that Dave and Millie were arguing about whether either of them should do the same. He'd heard them. Lately Dave had spent more time in his own cottage and cooked more of his own meals.

Sam himself was spending more time with Rory. But when he called at the house on a Saturday a few days after Lia's letter arrived, he found him packing.

"We're definitely moving back," Rory told him, once the two of them were out of the house and on the way to the beach.

"Why?"

"My dad has to leave."

"Has to? Why?"

He shrugged, and kicked a pebble.

"He was sent here. We didn't really live on a community."

"What?"

"I'm not supposed to say anything, but as they keep telling me, I'm a head case. They think so at the school too. The sooner I get back on the chill program the better."

"Do you want to get back on it? Do you want to leave?"

"Not really. Not now. You can get used to stuff..." He smiled. "Even crap. People have been... Jameson has been annoying, but, you know... alright, for a bozo. " He paused. "So have you."

"I don't get it," said Sam, noticing the semi-compliment after it had been thrown away. "Why do you have to go? Is your dad a tabloid journalist or something? Are there front page scandals about us in the papers?"

"Don't think so. He hates journalists. He hates most people, especially me. I never used to see him before. He was always at work, away a lot. I know he didn't want to come. He told my mum it was pointless. She just says he can't talk about his job. He's not allowed."

Rory could see from Sam's face that he felt sorry for him and he wasn't having it.

"Bad stuff makes you tough," he claimed. "Sharpens you up. You could do with some."

"I had more than enough," said Sam, "thanks."

Sam saw it sink in, saw the sorry that would never make it from Rory's face to his throat. But Sam was still processing Ken Fielder. He nearly asked whether he was a spy, but it sounded too stupid in his head. Anyway, they were leaving, and it didn't seem fair on him. Besides, he was just beginning to think Rory was alright and not such a total psycho after all.

"Tell you what, though," said Rory, animated suddenly, "do you think that now I've been on the BBC and, you know, a bit of a celebrity, I could get a recording contract out of it?"

"Not until you stop chucking the guitar around and learn to play it."

Rory took that kind of thing from him now, sometimes, if he was in the right mood, with the Christmas concert applause in his head. He threw a pebble out to sea, but it wasn't much of a skimmer, so he kicked some more. Then he brightened as he looked up.

"Talking of T.V. stars, is it true? About that Matt guy being Robbo's dad? His real dad?"

"What? Don't be stupid."

The old scowl came back then, but Sam was too worried about Robbo to care about winding Rory up.

"That's why he wasn't in school yesterday, dummo. He's not ill. He won't want to see you," Rory told him, in a tone that questioned Sam's intelligence.

"We'll see," said Sam, already on the way towards the cottages and Robbo's place.

"They'll want to be left alone," Rory called after him.

Sam remembered the things he'd heard about Hazel crying all the time, and the visitor from the mainland who didn't want to turn round and go away again. It all began to make a strange kind of mixed up sense. Poor Robbo. Sam had to try to be a friend even if he didn't want one right now.

As he hurried further away from Rory, he heard him shout something that he couldn't quite make out. Something like, "My dad's got a gun." But the wind carried it away. He must have misheard.

Staring at the screen in the school office, Darius O'Dell was hoping he might have misread something somewhere. But specs or no specs, and for all the gobbledygook, the message only had one meaning.

Since the documentary had highlighted the existence of the one surviving school in Britain that had not been linegraded, and since the viewers had seen for themselves the kind of behaviour tolerated in that school, the writing, gobbledygook and all, had been on the wall. This latest ae mail was to inform him that the process of restructuring would begin as soon as possible.

At the emergency meeting Freya, the Head Girl, asked what it would mean.

"Sam can tell you quite a lot," she said, "because Lia has told him."

He half-expected someone to say that Lia had caused quite enough trouble already, but nobody did. He told them everything he could remember, from the computers for every child ("Cool man!" from Erik) to the chilling by medication if necessary.

And from the Behaviour Police ("No way!") to the lack of real teachers ("What about if you're upset? What about if a little one wants a cuddle?")

"Do we have a choice?" asked Freya.

"Yes!" cried Sam. "We always have a choice."

Millie stared, and put her arm through his. Then Beaky rose up from the bench on which she had been listening, grave and intent.

"Yes, Sam, we do. Unlike poor Lia I have not experienced linegraded education first-hand, but I have read a good deal about it, more than enough to make me want to spit." (Giggles from Erik.) "We cannot consider surrendering our precious freedom to a system that seeks not to educate, but to process children. It's a system that has no respect for individuality or creativity and places no value on joy."

"Yeah!" cried Sam, and decided not to feel silly.

"I am assuming," said Darius, that we will resist...by all means possible, and peaceful. We'll fight it."

They were agreed.

As they dispersed, subdued but tense with adrenalin, Dave told Sam that if he was planning to steal his phone, forget it.

"Call her," he said, producing it from his top pocket. "She's a witness."

Mentally, Dave added that Lia might like to mention to that father of hers that as it was all down to him, he owed them – all the help that money, power and those famous names he dropped could deliver. But that was a different call.

Sam took the phone to the beach, and listened to the relentless cold grey waves that separated them from the mainland as he talked to her. She didn't say a word until he'd finished. Looking closely at the tiny picture of her stretched out on her bed, he saw that she was crying.

"Lia?"

"What can I do?"

"Are you good with hopeless causes?"

"Sam, no! Never do that. How can it be hopeless when we're going to fight it together? You know what my dad said to your mum?"

"That she had beautiful eyes? Made fabulous scones?"

"Sam! He said we're an unbeatable force…or something like that. And we are. Ask Shadow."

"Sorry, he can't come to the phone. His mouth is full of oats."

"Idiot!" she spluttered. "Why are you trying to be funny?"

"Well, you were crying. It's my school, my community…and you were crying."

"Because you can't really know what you'd lose. I know. I already lost it, remember? Nobody fought to keep it, not even me, and I still miss it."

"Freedom?"

"Yes, that too. You don't appreciate it because you've always had it. But not just that. That isn't all they'll take away, if you let them."

He could see the little lines of concentration on her forehead but her eyes were still full, and spilling. Remembering that this wasn't his phone, Sam, told her he must go, sent his love to Charlie and said goodbye.

Lia wiped away her tears and stared into her interactive mirror at the face that looked so hurt. She clicked thoughtlessly through each angle while she searched for the word she needed, the word that summed up what the system would take, if they let it. It was a name for being alive, really alive, and unique, but sharing that life in common with other human beings.

Yes. It was humanity, and it was worth fighting for.

Twenty

In all their years of experience, the team behind the linegrading of the last school in Britain had never had to plan and execute such a simple, yet impossible task.

On the one hand there were so few cubicles to be erected, so few computers to install and kickwire, and such a limited number of staff to be recruited to do it. And given that this was a Level Three restructuring, they were dispensing with some of the extras, like the covered playcentre, piped music and disinfected air.

On the other hand, the island was…well, an island, across a miserable stretch of sea. Given the lack of a hotel or even a pub, there was a feeling that the quicker the job could be done the better.

Decca Quinn didn't fancy it much. She liked her little luxuries. But she couldn't see it taking more than four days. Then it wouldn't be long before the schools that had been first on the list needed an upgrade, because technology never stood still.

Decca's pre-teen kids, Kim and Troy, had bought her what they called a kit: some beads, bells and incense, and a silk flower that would look ridiculous in her short, sleek hair. They didn't usually find her work so amusing.

A fleet of white vans headed for the coast, where at Greatport they transferred to an old ferry coaxed out of retirement. The short crossing was quite long enough for the stomachs of the linegrading crew on board, as they huddled below deck groaning at the lurching swell of the winter waves, buffeted by a ferocious wind.

Trying to cheer one another with chat, they had no inkling that this spot of trouble with the elements was nothing but a spat in comparison with the struggle ahead of them. But the moment they could see the island through mist and spray, and hear it too, through the crashing and splashing all around them, they began to understand.

Along the beach by the jetty, holding hands and singing loudly and slowly, "We will overcome, We will overcome, We will overcome some day…" was the scruffiest, hairiest and most colourful crowd of people their work had ever obliged them to face.

Holding hands to form a human chain, they stretched along the pebbles, some attached to goats and some accompanied by crooning dogs attempting to join in the protest song.

Decca couldn't help noticing a rather magnificent black carthorse standing patiently, while two children, one with spiky red hair and the other milky black and stunning, sat one behind the other on its back, without saddle or bridle. They were returning her gaze with an intensity that made her look away.

"What the hell..?" began Mikey, who was too old for trouble and thinking of making this job his last.

"Sacré bleu!" murmured Yves, who was only half French but found it more satisfying in moments of high drama.

"Nobody warned us about this," muttered Lulu, but she was grinning.

She liked a challenge, and the pharma-counsellor in her was intrigued, because they looked so calm, so chilled, and so totally focused.

"You have got to be kidding!" breathed Decca. She knew this boat was from another era, but she hadn't expected it to take them back in time. "This must be how the Romans felt when they landed on the Kent coast. But they didn't stand any nonsense either. A few skirmishes and the locals knuckled down and learned what was good for them."

"But if memory serves correctly, boss," said Ahmed, "that was only after they'd burned down London, St Albans and Colchester – and slaughtered several thousand savages who probably looked a bit like that lot there!"

Decca pointed out how few of them there actually were, and that according to the last census, most were under eighteen or over fifty. Besides, as Ahmed recalled, they were pacifists who could only protest without violence of any sort.

"So any resemblance to ancient warriors is more of a fashion statement than anything else," smiled Lulu.

The crew couldn't help a certain amount of nervous grinning as they climbed down to the jetty. Ahead of them the chain remained unbroken.

When the singing stopped and the crowd fell silent, it was with perfect synchronicity, like a choir.

Now the crew had to tackle the slippery but savage pebbles, while from the boat the drivers threw down a ramp to smooth a way for the vans. Each step, in brand new top of the range walking boots, sounded explosive in their ears as they crunched towards the gathered human silence.

"Are you going to make way, or watch as we walk round you?" asked Decca, trying to sound confident but not threatening.

She could in fact see both ends of the line. The island might be small, but there was no way its inhabitants could ever encircle it. The gesture was symbolic only, and pointless.

Lia and Sam watched as Beaky reached out a hand towards the woman at the front of the group.

"Welcome to Rainbow Dreams."

Decca shook the offered hand, but looked uncomfortable.

"It's a disquieting kind of welcome."

"We bear you no personal animosity. You have been sent to do a job. We simply wish to make it clear that it's a task we cannot allow you to accomplish, and to give you the opportunity to turn back now."

"That won't be possible."

"On the contrary, it is the linegrading of our school that will prove to be impossible," countered Beaky, "as you will discover."

Sam was finding it hard not to whoop his support and admiration. But they had agreed on their goal: the overwhelming strength of dignity.

If the team thought that the greeting would herald a graceful parting to allow them through, they were mistaken. Beaky mended the break in the chain at once. They saw that though they could find a way off the beach, it would be both noisy and painfully slow.

It was only when the heavy vans had ground their way onto sand that the human chain disbanded, at a signal from Garth. Then the islanders walked slowly away, resuming their song as they scattered onto higher ground.

Sam glanced at the ferry, turning around to begin its voyage back to obscurity. It made him smile that this hi-tech team had been dependent on such a crock. He couldn't help wondering, though, whether the ugly but tough old boat would have survived the storm that killed his father. And he wished his dad were there to join them, to make him stronger.

As it was, that seemed to be Lia's job. She had been dropped off not much more than an hour ago, in an old heliplane hired by her mother. Her father, in fact, would only learn where she had gone when he returned from work, but she'd assured him that her mum would smooth it. He owed her.

Some of the brothers and sisters had had very little idea what they were fighting against until she'd told them. She'd been so full of fire, they'd all caught a spark, and some of them were calling her Emmeline after the Suffragette leader who'd won women the vote.

Sam knew Rory was pretty smitten with her. He couldn't blame him. He couldn't even feel sorry that the Fielders were still there, because Ken had had some good ideas to throw in at the big meeting the night before. Whatever his job was, he didn't seem in any great hurry to get back to it.

When the protesters appeared to be scattering, they were not in fact separating into their own cottages, but advancing on the school, where the chain reformed. Unlike the island, it was just about small enough to be encircled all the way round. Already equipped with provisions, it was ready to become their base, their HQ for the campaign, however long it had to last.

Predictably, it had been Beaky who had insisted that they made education the focus of the sit-in. The plan was to let the day unfold like any other school day, but to hold each lesson outside in the open air. It would be an opportunity, she said, for the older people to retrieve some the learning they had lost.

There were scouts on shifts, keeping the chain informed of where the linegraders were and what they were doing. For the rest of the adults, it was Beaky-style maths, followed by poetry, then art, and football practice.

Isabel, who at eighty-one was the oldest member of Rainbow Dreams, said she thought she'd rather like to join Class One with Miss Lane. She liked the sound of the chance to play in the Wendy House and give voices to the glove puppets.

Some, on the other hand, were confident enough to opt for the teenage curriculum with Mr Jameson, who promised not to push them too hard with the physics or geometry.

Millie was heading the refreshments team based in the school kitchen. There had been enough baking to keep up energy levels for days. But because the February morning was bitingly crisp in spite of its glow, Dave was going to need to slot in extra P.E. in quick, temperature-raising bursts.

And should spirits flag, music would revive them. The school supply of instruments had been supplemented from many homes, and the piano from the hall wheeled out through the front door and covered with blankets to keep it warm.

So they were ready, and when Decca left the rest of her team erecting two portakabins in order to investigate, one look at the children's faces told her it was also irresistible fun. Adults should know better – and might, if they took a hesitant step into the real world.

"A temporary stalemate," was what Decca called it, hoping none of her colleagues would ask her to identify the move that would change the game.

At the end of a day in which they had achieved absolutely nothing, the image that lingered in Decca's head as she tried to sleep had little to do with sweetness and light.

As she rolled from one side to another she pictured the theatrics of the pretty boy whose name was the first they had learned. Earlier that day he had pretended to throw a slo-mo bomb of some kind, whirling like a demented fast bowler before delivering it, and then exploding his own body in a leaping, writhing exhibition with sound effects. Followed by laughter – his own, and not very nice.

So much for love and peace. The boy was a yob, a thug, a sicko. Lulu could waste her pharma-counselling expertise on a case like that; personally Decca would strap him down for a bit of brain restructure.

In the school, too wired for sleep, Sam remembered it too.

"What was that all about?" he wanted to know.

He had come in on the climax as Rory re-gathered his limbs and extracted bits from his hair.

"Creative self-expression," said Rory. "You lot are big on that."

"This is serious," Sam told him. "You'll be gone but this is our way of life. Don't give them what they want."

"What difference does it make?" Rory wanted to know. "They think you're loonies. I can give them loony."

Lia appeared with drinks. It was eight hours in to the protest and the sun was paling. Sam reminded her, with a nod up to the still-blue sky, that he'd said it wouldn't rain.

"Not water, no," said Rory, "but man is the shit gonna come down!"

Lia had decided to do what her parents tried with Charlie when he thought it was funny to be unsavoury, and pretended he wasn't there.

"You're the one who's always right about everything," Sam told her, ignoring Rory's impression of him as lovestruck sap.

"Well, I've been right today. They didn't do anything. Nothing at all. They've got no plan. See, we've got two things they lack: a cause and a strategy. How can we lose?"

"I wanted to do the night shift," complained a still-present Rory, "but it's sorted. Do you think that's what they're waiting for – a night attack?"

"Doesn't matter if they are," said Sam. "We'll be ready."

"Suppose they send in the SAS?"

"What? Don't be stupid! Against unarmed peace activists?" Lia retorted, but it was a new thought that shocked her.

Rory was a little hurt by her derision. He muttered that she didn't seem to realise how low these people might sink.

"Who'd know?" he continued. "I bet no one outside the DOLE knows they're here. Where are the reporters covering it for The News? They'd have to behave themselves if there were cameras here."

"Oh yeah, like you did! And it was such a great success last time!" Lia couldn't help reminding him. "You're not planning on throwing any linegrading computers around before they can be kickwired, are you?"

His eyes lit up.

"Into the sea?"

"No, Rory. Not part of the plan. Too destructive," Sam told him. "From the fishes' point of view."

"That's his trouble," said Rory, nodding towards Sam. "He always sees everything from the fishes' point of view," and he began to slouch off, mouthing fishily for the benefit of Lia, who couldn't help laughing.

"That boy gets weirder," she smiled.

"Yeah, I told you he was starting to fit in."

"But I'll be right about the shit, you'll see," shouted Rory from the school doorway, and added, in a big stage whisper, "That reminds me – I must beg for more of that delicious lentil soup."

After supper, everyone sang, and those who weren't too full managed a spot of dancing. Some of Kara's small pupils held her hands and danced, holding on to legs and skirt edges when the hands ran out. Garth and Dave had laid a fire which was roaring by the time the darkness would have been at its deepest and coldest.

The night plan involved half the adults and teenagers going home to their own cottages to do some more baking and stock up on sleep. The other half would stay on, and sleep inside the school, taking turns on sentry duty. Two would stay close to the kabins and the vans outside them, to watch for suspicious noises or movement. At last Dave no longer felt a vague guilt at possessing a phone. Old mobiles like his were helping sentries around enemy HQ to keep in touch.

Lia had promised she would call home every night.

"Did the school believe I'm sick?" she asked her mum.

"I doubt it. If they threaten us with prison we'll have to hope your dad's famous friends can front the campaign! Are you alright, Lia? You're not in any kind of danger, are you?"

"Not unless you count the danger of indigestion from Sam's lemon drizzle cake."

She smiled at him as she said it. He tried to pull his knitted hat over her face to stop her saying anything equally cheeky, so there was a certain amount of squealing and breathlessness. She escaped to take the call in private, sticking her tongue out at him as she disappeared into the darkness.

"Mum, can you get Dad to....well, alert the media? We must be making news here. Tell him to use his contacts, but Mum, don't let him come over. Please."

Roz said she didn't suppose he could count on much of a welcome. But she promised to pass on the message, even though she had hardly seen Carl since she dropped Lia on the island. She did not mention his outrage, the slammed door, and a silent breakfast.

Roz herself was too worried to sleep. She was clinging to Charlie tighter and longer than usual every time she hugged him. Personally, she wasn't at all sure that developments on the island would be considered newsworthy until somebody got hurt.

"Love to Charlie, Mum. And Blancmange. And Dad too. Tell him what I said, and tell him I'm fine, and I ticked off at least a hundred and twenty-four objectives today."

Returning to Sam, Lia found he had been joined by Robbo. She nearly made the enormous gaffe of asking after his mum, but remembered that apparently it was his dad – who was not actually his dad – who had left the island, and that a stranger called Matt had stayed to get to know his brand new son. She must congratulate her own father on that one.

Poor Robbo didn't look as if he'd slept much for days. The three of them were all staying in the school that night, with others including Millie, Dave, Ken Fielder, Sven, Christy and Beaky. Matt was there too, and seemed to be working hard at getting his son to talk to him, or even to look him in the eyes. Robbo seemed keen to lay his blanket as far away from his new father as possible.

A sulky Rory had gone home with his mother and promised to write a protest song to teach them all in the morning. Sam had anticipated the chorus in his best Rory impression, twenty-first century Dylan with even weirder tuning:

"Oh I..I..I just wanna stay with you, babe...I don't want to leave you tonight....no no no"

"Oh funny!" grinned Lia, threatening to punish him with a smelly sock in the face, but he grabbed it and threw it at her.

"You're like a brother and sister," said Robbo.

"I know," said Lia.

"Yeh," said Sam. "We can't stand each other."

The hall floor didn't give them the best night's sleep of their lives. The worn old gym mats smelt rubbery but had little spring. But Sam, who had been known to sleep, just for a change, in a field or on the beach, dropped off first. So he was unaware of Rory returning to the hall and slipping into a corner, guitar in hand, hushing the twang it made when he knocked it against a cupboard.

Lia heard the unplayed chord through the vagueness of almost-sleep as she stretched out between Millie and Beaky. For a long time it had felt like she was the only one left awake, listening to the breathing of the others, and a certain amount of snoring.

She did think, a while later when she woke with a cold and sore shoulder, that she heard someone move, and go outside, inviting in a blast of thick, cold air that made her pull her blanket tighter up to her chin until she found out how badly it tickled. She hadn't known blankets still existed.

If she had been alert enough to think it through, she would have remembered that the night watch sentries were sleeping in the corridor, so as not to disturb the rest at two hourly intervals. There must, then, be another explanation, but at the time her brain was finally tiring as her heavy body had long ago begun to do.

She heard no more. Instead she was riding Shadow into the waves, a pure white horn on his head piercing a hole in each towering, crashing wall, until he turned into a holographic horse of foam, tossing her into the wild water and down, down into the coldest, darkest depths of the ocean.

Rory had heard the movement, seen the crack of moonlight and followed the figures through it. He had an idea that one of them was his father, and whatever he was doing he wanted to be in on it – or stop it. It was impossible to know, with his dad.

It was very, very dark outside. He had thought they would have torches, whoever they were. Of course if they were RD they had probably developed night vision along with all their other Men Of Nature weirdnesses, but he could hardly see a step ahead.

"Dad, wait for me!"

How limp did that sound! It was pitiful. Rory was glad to learn from the silence that the feeble infant voice had got lost in it. But he was going to have to go it alone, do it alone, whatever it was. What was the word? Sabotage.

Pretty stupid of the linegraders to illuminate themselves the way they did, with their fear of this total darkness, like children who needed an open door and the landing light left on through the night. It was a long way off, but he could see it like a big star in the blackness. And it meant their vans were right there, asking for it.

He'd put the nails in his pocket earlier, when the inspiration had visited. He felt them, their ridges and hardness, and pushed the point of one into a hand until it hurt. The hiss of tyres was a sound that pleased him. He'd heard it before. Would she be proud of him?

Something moved down by his feet. Something live and fluttery, something sudden, jerking and twisting, something that should be medicated. His elbows bent to protect his face from wings that might lift and brush his cheek, but there was nothing. Whatever it was, it had gone. Wuss. Get a grip.

His shoe slid, in mud or worse. Swearing, he steadied himself, only to stub his toe on something sharp and hard. This place! Why would anyone want to save it from anything?

Rory felt the coldness of the air on his cheek now, burning his ears. His arms reached out in front of him, hands raised like a blind man, feeling in the nothingness. Afraid. He was afraid. And he didn't like it. It was worse than the needles, the pills, the eyes closed for therapy, the calm voices trying to break into his mind.

The noise was so sudden he thought his heart was going to escape through the wall of his chest. Familiar but loud, breathy, now behind him, now above his head, flying like the hooves that held him still, trapped by fear, the air moving around him as he smelt it, full of horse sweat and horse breath. It was so big, so unchilled and heavy, and hidden in the darkness. Except for a brief, noisy moment of teeth.

Rory could not move. He dug a nail in, deep, into his palm, but it didn't help.

"Shoo!" he tried. "Get out of it, you brute!"

The child was back to shame him with the little voice. Still the animal beat and pounded, twisted and turned like a demented whirlwind, and still his feet clung fast to the earth.

By the time it left him alone he had nothing left in the silence but the fear. Rory turned and slowly retraced his steps back to the school, glad to feel the door against his wrist, to smell the food in the air, to hear someone snoring.

Lia stirred. He was sure it was her, recognised something in the murmur she made, wished he could see her face.

"Rory?" she whispered.

He had stood no stiller with the horse charging around him. The density of all the breathing from the floor was reassuring. She would think she dreamed him. Pleased with the thought, Rory found a space and tried to fit into it. And fell asleep eventually, one hand wrapped around the nails.

Twenty-One

Sam woke around dawn, when someone tripped over him on the way to the toilet. He felt sweaty, bad-breathed and achy, but his adrenalin kicked in the moment he remembered where he was and why. There was a damp heat in the hall, thanks to all those wrapped bodies, some of them still sleeping. He soon saw, though, that Lia was not among them, and found her in the school kitchen with Millie, helping to stir a very large pan of porridge.

"I was just telling your mum how you kept everyone awake all night with your snoring," she told him by way of a greeting.

Remembering the momentary moonlight that had been let into the hall along with the cold during the night, Lia told them what she had heard, but it sounded lame. Soon after breakfast, however, it became a lot more interesting when Sven reported back to base that the linegrading crew had surfaced, but seemed to have lost something important.

"Yes," said Ken Fielder, "it seems that some crucial bits and pieces, which would help them to assemble the cubicles and kickwire the computers, have somehow disappeared from their vans in the middle of the night."

"That's odd," said his accomplice Paris, lifting his eyes to the ceiling and away from Christy's opening mouth.

"I wondered where you...." she began.

"How very mysterious," said Ken.

Sam and Lia exchanged glances that acknowledged some guilty secret between these two unlikely allies. It struck Sam that though one was greyer and a lot less personable than the other, they were both still newcomers in a community that would never sanction such freelance action without consensus. The two of them were like naughty schoolboys who were so pleased with their secret prank that they really wanted to own up and take the credit.

"What have you done with them, Dad?" cried a delighted Rory. "Hey, why didn't you let me come with you? I could break into a van – if you taught me."

"I'm afraid my son lives in a fantasy world," smiled Ken to the expectant audience. "Now what would I do with all those little essential bits and pieces? I could hardly flush them down the loo."

"Milk the moment, Dad!" cried Rory, trying to slap the palm of an unpresented hand. He was finding the situation funnier by the second. "I'm proud of you. Bit of a first, eh? But then, I suppose you've never been proud of me at all."

Sam saw Lia wince. She was sorry for him, poor Rory. And perhaps she should be. He should be too.

"Why don't you go down to the kabins with a megaphone?" muttered Ken.

"Oh, sorry," came Rory's stage whisper, "is it TOP SECRET?"

"Well, wherever the stuff has got to, they're going to be a bit stuck without it all," said Dave. "If they had a Plan A, which didn't seem too obvious yesterday, they're going to need to think up Plan B pretty quickly."

In the kabin, which Decca had found increasingly claustrophobic through the night, the mood was not exactly upbeat. She was cross with herself because she had thought she heard something out there, but then there was a lot out there to hear. It was all disturbingly unfamiliar: the sea, the wind, and all kinds of animals and birds best injected and then confined to wildlife parks. If she'd investigated every one she would have had no sleep at all.

As Day Two began with another setback she felt cross, too, with the powers that be, for sending her out to this place with no warning that the job was going to be a waking nightmare.

"It's theft," grumbled Yves. "Breaking and entering. Where are the police on this island?"

"They've never needed any cops. They've never had any crime."

"We can certainly send for more parts," agreed Decca. "But do we really want a criminal investigation that could get us in the papers? If anyone interviewed that woman with the nose, she'd fire up every intellectual in Britain. There's more than a few, you know, against the whole program."

A bemused silence followed while they shook their heads and muttered about the trouble-making of the writers, artists, musicians and philosophers who questioned the merits of linegrading.

"So what do we do today, apart from wait for a delivery? Count animal droppings? Go apple picking? It's a bit nippy for a swim," said Mikey.

"We could evacuate the school," said Ahmed.

"Tear gas?" grinned Mikey.

"Very helpful, Michael. Thanks for that," said Decca, but had to admit she had no ideas.

Maybe a walk would bring inspiration – if her lungs could face the challenge. The air was so thick she could taste it. God knew the bacteria it might carry, the spores. She braved the breeze and pulled up her hood, heading briskly past the cottages and farms to check on the lunatics at the school.

Decca noticed the earthy smell that clung in the chill air with a hint of manure causing her to wrinkle her nose in disgust. It was odd how many flower borders and vegetable patches looked and smelt freshly dug. Anyone would think these people did their gardening at night.

At the school several people waved and said good morning. The red-haired woman even offered her porridge, which she declined in a knee-jerk of a moment, only to feel ridiculous.

"Arsenic-free, honest!" claimed the wild-looking boy who really did need an intense course of psycho-chilling, and whose grin made the porridge much easier to resist.

Perhaps the reflex had not been so stupid. They were a kind of enemy, and she wasn't here to consort with them. They had wasted enough of her time already.

"I see you've been tending your crops in the night," she told them, the tone meant to warn them she was wise to their childishness, and not amused.

"Planting," said Beaky. "The seeds of change – and I rather suspect they will grow, spread and flourish, until they flower all over Britain."

Sam and Lia exchanged triumphant smiles. Beaky for Prime Minister! Surely this woman could right wrongs, overturn governments and free the world with a turn of phrase! But Indira Bird was not altogether happy with the lawlessness of the night raid, and said they needed to establish lines which they must all agree not to cross.

Meanwhile Decca had returned to her own base, where all the others had rustled up for breakfast was seal-packed toast.

"Okay," she told them, "This is where it gets serious. I've called about the parts and I've also explained to our bosses exactly what we are up against. They have promised to call me back...."

"When they've thought of something!" finished Mikey, crunching crisps and reflecting that with nothing to do, he was getting through his illicit store of black market red label snacks rather too quickly.

"Yes," said Decca. "That's their job. Thinking. And until they do, we can't do ours. It's actually going to be a beautiful day. I think I'm going to go for proper walk this time, all around this island, every inch of it. You never know what I might find."

Lulu decided to go with her. Mikey decided to go back to bed. Yves decided to hunt around in the vans, to see if their night visitors had left him anything he could work with, even if all he could achieve was assembling a few cubicles.

Ahmed, the technical mastermind, began to investigate whether he could still kickwire the base computer with a kit he kept in his rucksack. Sometimes it was useful to be a nerd.

Outside the school the mood ebbed and flowed. At times it was buoyant, especially when the sun came out from behind the clouds and decided to stay a while, but never relaxed. The buzzword was wary.

"Fear complacency. Delete picnic in the park, Reading Festival. Remember Vietnam, Iraq, the voice unheard, the gesture futile. Watch. Pray. Suspect, anticipate, outmanoeuvre. And above all," said Beaky, "believe."

Rory cheered so loudly that Sam spared a little of that suspicion for him. But it seemed he was waiting for his moment, found it hard, and rushed it anyway. Addressing the audience Beaky had held captive, he presented his protest song, delivered with all the star quality he could muster. It had a fast and sliding chorus that veered off in a different musical direction every time, and that no one else could pin down. But the words were easier to remember:

You think that you can plug us in
But that don't mean you'll ever win
Or understand what being free

Has just begun to mean to me
You think that you can take control
But you will never wire my soul

Lars tried to turn it into a kind of hip hop rap, which sounded funny in a Swedish accent. Beaky showed on the school piano that it worked very well as a slow and stately Victorian hymn, which was somehow even funnier. And even though the composer protested, and insisted that the original version was best, he loved all the attention.

"Well?" he asked Sam, as they kicked a ball around at the back of the school. "Classic or what?"

Sam pretended to weigh up the two options and wondered what Rory would do if he opted for the what. He found himself smiling.

"Well," he said, "it's not quite… crap."

Rory let loose an enormous roar of a laugh which might have sent any nearby chickens squawking for cover.

"Only when you sing it!" he said when it had stopped.

Sam would have denied trying, but Rory's pointing finger told him he'd been caught. Both boys grinned, and Sam realised that he had never liked Rory quite as much as he did in that moment – no one else around, no apologies or admissions, no Lia. It wasn't quite friendship, but whatever it was, it felt better. It felt okay.

Later he was given permission to slip out to fetch Shadow, to serve as a focus for maths problems about how many kilograms of oats he could eat in a month, how long it would take him to gallop around the perimeter of the island, and how many chickens would be needed to balance him on giant scales. But of course it was also to stop boy and horse pining for each other.

At the other HQ, most of the learning taking place that day involved dealing with setbacks. Yves could not begin to assemble the individual pupil plug-in stations, because many of the plastic panels stacked flat in the vans turned out to be missing.

On their return from their walk, red-cheeked and unusually tousled, Decca and Lulu were able to explain. At the open-air church, new shelters, painted with flowers, peace signs, doves and yes, rainbows, offered a rainy day alternative to grass and rock. Arranged in a circle all around like a mini Stonehenge, but rather more psychedelic, the panels had also presumably proved much quicker to erect by the light of dawn.

"We knew they were big on recycling," said Lulu, but Decca's scowl rejected all humour.

Lulu did not add that it was a special place, although she felt oddly chilled. "It's not like any other church I've ever seen. Our panels are the only things there that aren't part of Nature."

Decca observed that the islanders had done their best to make them look as if they were. She didn't understand either of them, art or nature. Or God, either, come to that. Decca liked things she could install, run, shut down. Until now there had never been anything that troubleshooting could not disarm.

Ahmed appeared to explain that he had managed to kickwire the central computer independently, but only to find that there was something wrong with it, something which could be a virus, or the work of a very clever hacker.

Whenever it was turned on, a rainbow crossed the screen and didn't want to disappear whatever he tried. And a rather whiningly tuneless song about taking control, being free and wiring up the soul droned along on a loop which was hard to stop, and even harder to erase from the memory – of the hardware, or the brain.

"I can't get past them to do anything," he complained, the sigh long with frustration.

It was lost on none of them that the same could be said of the hippies at the school. And they had no way of knowing how much frustration the young hacker had contended with, how many shouts and clenched fists had made way for triumphalist arm-dancing when the luck clicked in.

But soon Decca had better news of her own. At least, she hoped it was good. They had not been abandoned. Her boss, who finally returned her call, assured her that reinforcements were on the way. Who they were, or what their instructions might be, they would have to wait and see.

The others were relieved – apart from Mikey, who was nowhere to be found.

A tour of the island yielded nothing, no sign of him. His phone was apparently malfunctioning and his red label food store appeared untouched. Ahmed suggested looking to alcohol for the explanation, but Decca pointed out that time, or the memory of it, might disappear in that way, but not people. Mikey was a very large man to lose on such a tiny island.

She would have to enlist the help of the loonies in the morning. Unless...

No. Not even the wild boy. Surely.

But Decca could not sleep. She woke Ahmed, Yves and Lulu and ventured out in the unnerving blackness to demand the truth.

Twenty-Two

It was Beaky who first saw the contingent from the portakabins and ushered them in a whisper into the school kitchen, doors closed on to the hall where most were fast asleep.

"I am incredulous," she said, at the end of Decca's speech, "at what I suspect you may be implying. Perhaps you would like to inspect the kitchen cupboards for rifles? Or attend a science lesson, to satisfy yourselves that the brewing up of chemical weapons is not on the curriculum?"

Decca regretted the sleepiness which had made her less than tactful. She added hastily that she was accusing no one of anything – well, at least not of that – and that she simply wanted to find this missing member of her team.

Beaky promised to do what she could, woke Garth and Paris, and accompanied the linegraders on a torchlit search, but had to admit, two hours later, that it was very odd. The man simply seemed to have vanished.

By breakfast the news had spread through the school.

"Maybe he ran out of junk food," Rory suggested, eating between Sam and Lia, "and swam off to Greatport to top up his store. His heart gave out and he's feeding the fishes now. For at least a month."

Lia frowned at Sam.

"What?" cried Rory. "Do you think I cut him up to give the fishes a hand?"

"You haven't locked him in the stock cupboard for a laugh?" said Sam.

"He'd be happy enough as long as I left him enough red label treats," Rory pointed out. "I did consider it as an option, but there's no toilet in there and although I have been known to call the resources here crap…"

"Enough," said Lia. "I'm eating."

But Sam knew she never found him as tiring as he did, that she humoured him, missed the worst in him looking for the best. Maybe it was the only way.

Rory knew he'd pushed it further than he meant to. Did she think he was disgusting? Was he? Besides, he hadn't really made it clear that he was on their side. Standing with the La Las against the world he used to think he almost belonged to. Hippies against progress. He wasn't sure they would believe him anyway. He hardly believed himself.

And he needed to talk to his father. In private.

But consternation about the mysterious disappearance of Mikey Brown gave way sooner than anyone had envisaged to concern on a rather different scale.

The motor launch sent a full throttle warning of its arrival when it was still some miles out to sea. Interrupted in the middle of a kiss, Christy and Paris, who were on look-out duty close to the jetty, were slow to register what it meant. Decca, however, had been listening out for it and saw it first.

She was there, with the rest of the team, to read the word POLICE, and though she was not as outraged as the young parents-to-be, she was far from happy. She had been led to expect a unit of Security officers led by a psycho-negotiator, not cops who would presumably be armed.

Christy and Paris were running now, hand in hand. The launch was docking, and one after another the special response officers emerged, jumping onto the jetty and down to the pebbles.

It was with mixed feelings that Decca noticed the guns hanging from their belts. They were hard to miss.

The sergeant in charge of the unit was stocky, and walked with a slow swagger. He also had a wide smile, which he beamed on Decca, who didn't enjoy it.

"Sergeant Bill Hammond," he said, shaking her hand vigorously as he stepped up from the pebbles. "Don't panic, Ms Quinn. We're here to make a point. No one will be hurt."

"Is that what they said at the O.K. Corral?" asked Ahmed.

Decca told the sergeant about Mikey. He raised thick eyebrows and cracked the knuckles on one hand while considering the information.

"I wasn't told of any escalation."

Decca said she wouldn't use the word, had no proof, would rather not…but he interrupted, eyebrows lowered.

"You might be a believer in smoke without fire," he said, "but in my experience there's usually a hell of a blaze somewhere. You just have to find it."

The linegraders found themselves staring. His hand was on the handle of the weapon and his teeth, revealed in a wide smile, were dazzlingly white.

"In the meantime," he added, "I understand the law has been broken in other ways."

"Well," admitted Lulu, "in kind of a playful way. Well, until….if…"

"I don't think we discriminate between playful lawbreaking and any other kind," Hammond said, "but if it's a game, well, we can play along."

He was grinning again and Decca wished he would stop.

"What will you do?" she asked him.

"Whatever we need to do to re-establish law and order, so that you can get into that school and do the job you've been sent to do. And we'll find your missing colleague too."

"Good," said Decca, crisply, wishing she did not feel as if everything was so utterly beyond her control. "Thank you, officer."

The launch was moored with a couple of the officers still on board. The other four set off to search for Mikey Brown while Hammond invited himself to the men's portakabin for a debriefing.

Outside the school there was rather more emotion. Christy left the talking to Paris, and kept apologising for her flood of tears. Beaky understood.

"More than ever now," she told them all, "we must take care that our behaviour is beyond reproach. No more whimsical flirtations with law-breaking, however much fun some of us may have had. We must not give them the slightest justification to use force of any kind."

"Maybe just being here is reason enough," said Darius. "Perhaps we should go before they try to make us."

There was a stunned silence which left him to reflect that this was not the kind of Churchillian speech a Head should be making in a crisis.

"What, and give up, just like that? Invite them to come in and wire up our children?" cried Kara.

"No one wants to give up," said Garth.

There was a chorus of agreement to that.

"We can't just stand around and wait to find out what they're going to do," said Lia. "We've been...well, in control up to now. We mustn't lose it."

"But they've taken that control away from us!" cried Christy, as Paris tried to console her. "They have the power, the authority, the weapons."

"But it's our island," said Millie. "It's about our future and our beliefs. And we are together. They are just a few individuals who don't really care, any more than Decca and Lulu and the lads. It's just a job to all of them, but for us, it's our life. And that makes us strong."

"No, no..." said Ken Fielder, breaking into the murmurs of warm support for Millie's words. "I mean, sorry, Millie, I know what you're saying, but it's...it's what Rory would call ...la la. Woolly as your jumper. It's emotion versus hard reality. We're not in a Hollywood movie and moral authority won't defeat the men with the guns. I'm sorry. That's just the truth of it."

The silence was brittle. One of the dogs broke it, followed by a crying child who needed a sleep.

"How do you know?" demanded someone, but for a moment neither Sam nor Lia knew where the question came from. "It might!"

It was Rory. But the voice had lost something, Or found something else. He looked so young, suddenly, that Lia wanted to hold him. There was silence. No one was staring harder than his father, who shook his head and sighed till Rory turned his attention to the wall where Lia's smile couldn't reach him.

"Look, I'm not really one of you," muttered Ken apologetically. "Feel free to ignore my real-world cynicism. I'm just warning you. Don't let your idealism lead you into a dangerous place. Don't let this end badly."

"You do bad endings, don't you, Dad?" called Rory as his father left them to discuss their options.

He watched him, eyes so hard on his back they hurt. Then he followed, at a distance, turning to Lia with an exaggerated finger to the mouth, as if it was still a game he was playing. Secret agents, trailing, ducking into the shadows. As if he didn't care after all, about anything. Almost anything, she thought, and remembering the windblown kiss, looked away.

"All we can do is carry on," said Beaky. "We can't allow them to dictate our actions any more than they can dictate our beliefs."

"But can we still win?" asked Sam. "Mrs Bird, can we? Really?"

"I don't know, Sam," said Beaky, "but – and call me la la if you like – I don't see why not."

The cheering wasn't as rousing or as confident as it had been, before dawn, but it was enough to re-start the day. Rory told all the assembled pupils that they must be sure to remember Mrs Bird's request that she be renamed Lala, but Sam suspected that even he had more sense than to try it.

Concentration, when it came to geometry or the pyramids, map work or calligraphy, proved erratic. Sam's fruit loaf failed to tempt anyone but fans of burnt toast. But Rory was convinced his protest song was growing on his audience, even if no one was half as impressed as the composer himself. So when Freya returned from a stint of look-out duty outside the kabins and reported that she'd heard the skinny man singing it, he was exuberant.

"The one who looked like a computerhead," she explained, "but he didn't sing it the way you do, Rory, obviously."

"Obviously," beamed Rory, who didn't know that Ahmed would have paid good money to get that song out of his head.

So the mood at the school had already lifted a little by the time Sergeant Hammond and his men headed up to introduce themselves. Millie offered to fetch freshly-baked peanut cookies.

"Thank you, but we'll decline," said the sergeant, "unless you want the charges against you to be upped to manslaughter."

He let the silence run on a moment.

"I'm allergic, you see. I'd hit the floor in anaphylactic shock."

"Ah," said Millie. "Oh dear. I'm sorry."

"Kidding!" he said, and grinned, very broadly indeed.

Rory muttered something to Sam about a sick sense of humour.

"If we might return to the charges," prompted Darius O'Dell, who felt they were straying from a rather serious point, "what exactly would they be?"

"Breaking and entering into Department of Education vans. Criminal damage to government property. Theft of valuable equipment. That will be enough to be going on with for now."

"Charges against whom?" asked Beaky. "I presume you have individuals in mind. You don't wish to charge this child?"

She nodded to six-year-old Harry, who happened to be closest to the sergeant's legs, and was staring up at the weapons in his belt with puzzled fascination.

"Or my friend Isabel," she continued, putting her arm around the elderly woman, who looked frail in spite of her well known determination.

"Perhaps you would like to charge Gertie over there," she suggested, with a glance at the goat with its nostrils in the bucket of breakfast slops. "Or maybe you're inclined to pin the burglary on a cat."

Sam's mouth opened in admiration. Lia suppressed a snort. Robbo let his laugh go free.

Sven's wife Inge scooped up her tabby and stroked it protectively under the chin. Isabel's dog, which certainly wouldn't stand by while anyone arrested her, was beginning to sniff around and yap at the group of strangers. Laughter faded and smiles were cleared by the sudden grin that stretched across Hammond's face. Only to slacken grim in a blink.

"Look, I'm here to explain the situation as I see it," he began, as if his patience was wearing paper-thin. "We have no alternative but to arrest those guilty of the offences I've outlined."

"Not without evidence," said Dave.

"Evidence is not a problem. We can identify the culprits with DNA, but it will take a while. It would be simpler if the guilty parties stepped forward. Save all of us a lot of trouble."

"Dream on," said someone.

"Oh, I think you are the dreamers. The difficulty, really, is that those who have organised this illegal occupation of a government building – and obstructed the work of government employees – are guilty too. Even without DNA, I think we can work out who they are."

He aimed his grin at Beaky, at her headmaster, at Garth and Millie and Dave.

"So unless you leave quietly, and go back to your homes, we will be back to arrest not just the thieves, the artists, the lock-breakers and perhaps even the night-time gardeners....but also the leaders who are running this show."

He paused to renew the smile and shine it over a wider audience before he finished.

"Which will leave the protest in the hands of...let me see: the goat, the cat, the dog and of course, the children."

Lia felt too angry for tears, and cross with them for forming and stinging anyway as she stared fiercely at this grinning man with bright white teeth.

Even the dog had stopped barking.

"I'll let you think about it over lunch. You have until fourteen hundred," he continued. "That's two o'clock. When we will inform you about developments regarding the disappearance of Michael Brown and any further charges to be added."

The shock was palpable. There had been a hope, a certainty even, that the police would have found him by now, unharmed.

Sergeant Hammond had one last smile for them before he turned and led the others down the hill. Then he waved.

"See you guys later."

"Yeh," muttered Rory. "Not if we see you first."

Even in the night, the school had never been quite so silent.

Twenty-Three

They didn't anticipate much demand for lunch, but it had to be cooked. The team on the rota talked about carrots and beans when necessary, and arrests and surrenders when the subjects could no longer be avoided. Lars did suggest breaking into the chill supply, and injecting all the cops with an overdose of whatever they used these days to pacify troublemakers. Just for a moment they all enjoyed the image of police officers lying on the grass picking daisies and humming in the sunshine.

Millie was quiet. In her heart she felt it was over. It was hard to see what more they could do. She was worried sick about the fat man. And she didn't trust the policeman, with the toothy smile and that hand so close to the trigger. She didn't know how much further they could push Sergeant Hammond before he abandoned one and resorted to the other.

"Do you want any help, Mum?" asked Sam, wandering over.

"We're okay, love, thanks," she said, and put her arm round him. "Has anyone had a brainwave yet, found the obvious solution that nobody saw?"

He shook his head.

"Beaky's on look-out duty. She swapped with someone because she wanted a thinking space. Garth isn't saying much. Dave says there must be something we can do to wipe the smile off Sergeant Hammond's ugly face, but nobody knows what."

Millie's smile was pale, but brightened when she saw Lia approaching, asking if anyone had seen Rory.

"No, not for a while," Sam said flatly. "They could be leaving at last. Like his dad said, they don't really belong here."

Her frown questioned something in his voice that shocked him. He hadn't meant to sound as if he wanted them to go.

Rory had been so angry after the police left that Sam had half-expected him to pick up something to throw after them. He clearly remembered him doing the same sort of thing with much less reason, but that was a while ago now.

Was there something he had never worded, but found harder to forgive than the bruise? And did it matter? Sam thought he would be sorry now when he'd gone.

"I guess he won't have gone far without the guitar," said Faye.

She pointed out that it was still leaning against the piano, which Christy had just begun to play, very quietly and very slowly.

"What's the time?" asked Sam, as if to remind them all that there were more important questions to answer.

"Nearly thirteen hundred," said Lia, looking at her watch. "That's o'clock one to you dopey hippy types," she added with an impression of the Hammond grin.

"Yes, he's an arrogant man," said Millie, "but he's only doing his job. Technically, we have broken laws."

"Mum!" cried Sam. "You'd defend Sharkface?"

"Anyway," said Lars, "what about them? Henry says they're trespassing on our island."

"Nice try, but it doesn't work," said Sven, adding fresh basil to the bean hotpot. "The school does in fact belong to the Education Authority which is run by the state. Legally, it's not ours."

"So is there really nothing we can do?" asked Lia.

She had called her father, but didn't like to say so, in the circumstances. In any case, though he had promised to talk to his lawyer and media friends, he had told her not to be too hopeful.

"See what Indira has to say," said Millie, draining vegetables and leaning away from the steam. "If she can't find the answer, then there isn't one."

No one said it, but Sam couldn't have been the only one who reflected that Beaky couldn't even find a pretty substantial linegrader. No one was talking about what the police search might reveal.

"Where's Rory?" asked Lia suddenly.

"Never mind Rory," said Dave. "I keep thinking of the fat guy," and Sam wished he didn't keep picturing a body on a beach.

Rory was in fact with his father, sitting in the circle of stones up on the hill.

"So," Rory told his father, "tell me the truth. I know you never have."

Ken sighed. Rory knew he made him weary and depressed. He always had.

"You know the deal. I can only tell you what I'm allowed."

"And I used to think that was cool, in a weird way, but now I need to know – whether you know anything about Red Label Mikey."

"I know lots of things. That's my job. But if you're asking me whether I'm in any way responsible…"

"Yes, Dad, that's what I'm asking!"

Rory didn't want to look at his father's face. He stared instead, in the long silence, at the artwork on the cubicles that never were. But funky though it was, even if Sam had been involved, right now he couldn't really see it, the talent or the joke. What he could see was his father, tracking Mikey. Doing what he did best. Making himself invisible. Had he pushed his head underwater? Had he hit him, like he'd hit Rory more times than he could remember, but not just with the back of his hand – with something hard and heavy?

Sometimes he thought they were mad, these fantasies he dreamed up to fill the void that was his father. But sometimes they seemed more real than the cold, bald man at the sink or the kitchen table.

"It's all got out of hand, Rory. This place has got to me. I'm losing…something. My touch. My job, I dare say. My mind…"

"Helpful, Dad!"

"I don't know what you're asking."

"No," said Rory, springing up and throwing a clod of mud at a painted rainbow, "you never have."

The mud left on his hands was slimy. He spread out his fingers as he ran, and smeared it over his face, tasted it on his lips, spat, spluttered, heard his father's silence as he did not call his name, imagined the sigh.

And I've never asked you who you are, he called out in his head. They didn't know, either of them. And now, did either of them want to?

He ran all the way back to the school.

There lunch was being served without Beaky, and in something close to silence. Even the younger children, who did not understand what was happening, sensed the new mood among the adults. The meal was a sombre affair. Though there was plenty left in the pans, no one felt much like taking food down to the kabins, but Millie insisted.

Sam went with her, but their offer was declined by Decca and Lulu, who were sitting outside, but stopped talking as they approached.

"Police orders," said Decca.

"You lot have the drugs, not us," said Millie, looking towards the vans. "Or do they think the plan is to poison you all?"

"And bury the bodies in the vegetable gardens," added Sam.

Decca looked as if she had been shot.

"Mikey isn't actually dead," she said, "but that could change any minute if the paramedics don't make it over soon."

"What!"

"But...how? I don't understand...." began Millie, and Sam could tell she was about to cry.

"The police found him. It may have been a blow to the head."

The silence was thick as mist. Sam's chest hurt. It wasn't true. It was a conspiracy, like JFK and the grassy knoll. Only this time it wasn't some poor worker in a book depository who was being framed, but a whole community. A stitch-up! Maybe he never even disappeared. He'd been scoffing junk all this time, in the portakabin!

As he ran back to the school with his mother, he tried to tell her but she wasn't listening. Even when he asked her the time, all she said was, "Find Sven."

"But I don't believe it," Sam insisted. "Do you?"

"Things aren't lies, Sam, just because you don't want them to be true," she said, eyes straight ahead, scanning the crowd outside the building. "And it'll be two o'clock," she added, looking at her watch, "in twenty-eight minutes."

Twenty-Four

Everything was tangled now. Sam saw his mother find Sven, saw both their faces: the shock, the fear, the disbelief. Was this a good time to announce to the community that the bad news was that Mikey Scott was apparently dying? And the good news was that it could conceivably be a plot to discredit them all and turn everything around and over?

At quarter to two, possibly not. With nothing remaining but to join the quietness and add his silence to it, Sam realised he might cry if he knew what for. And his mother, the only one he could talk to, seemed to have left with Sven.

He saw that Rory was back, strumming the guitar for Lia's benefit. She noticed him coming and gave him an attempt at a brave smile. He returned it, equally weakly, but didn't muscle in, didn't want Rory's idea of humour, didn't want to have to lie to Lia with the truth withheld, or see in her face the damage it would do. He sat apart from them, busy looking somewhere else.

Lia and Rory kept an eye out for Beaky as they ate, but still she did not appear. Lia understood Sam's distance, if it was his way of getting through the minutes, but she wished he hadn't placed it between them. Not now.

It was almost two as she helped clear the dishes.

"Are you okay?" she asked, trying to take Sam's plate, but he wanted to see to his own and others' too.

Stupid question. She had hoped he would read the meaning inside it. Or in her voice, her eyes, something. In her hand, trying to help him before he rejected it.

Sam shook his head.

"They're coming," shouted someone.

All those who didn't already have a good view of enemy HQ came out as four officers advanced up the hill. Hammond led the way. He was in no hurry, his hair shining black with ridging gel, his gun dancing in sunlight as he swung one hip in front of the other.

The smaller children were gathered into adult arms. Isabel held her dog back this time, but though it couldn't snap round any uniformed legs, it yapped just the same. Rory's guitar stood with a twang, silenced against the piano. No one felt like singing. No one spoke, and for a long moment it felt as if no one moved.

The air was bright. Hands shaded foreheads. Sam caught a glint from a police weapon, a jab in the eye. Hammond took shades from his top pocket and placed them deliberately. The goat bleated.

"Rory, no!" came Lia's cry, as he bolted out from beside her, towards the cluster of cops.

In the left hand that had been brushing the guitar strings he clutched a gun, pulled out of a bag and pointed rather shakily at the policemen in general and Sergeant Hammond in particular. But all of them, the sergeant included, had drawn their weapons the moment they recognised his, so quickly that Lia, her eyes on

213

Rory, never even saw them reach. She felt silent sobs rise inside her as she stared. Four guns were aiming at Rory's head, the closest clasped in both hands by the sergeant, whose face bore no trace of a smile.

"Put the gun down, son," said Hammond, slowly and emphatically.

"Come back, lad!" called Garth. "That's not the way. That's not our way." He turned to the cops. "He won't shoot. It's probably not even loaded."

"It could be!" yelled Debs Fielder, her hands on her head, her voice breaking into a sob. "It could be."

Sam stared at his mum, who had covered her mouth, and at Lia, who stood rooted, lips parted, eyes glistening.

"We've had more practice with these things than you have, son," Hammond pointed out, as Rory glanced from one cop to another, his aim faltering, his right arm trying in vain to support the outstretched left and stop it wobbling. "We're all of us better at it than you are. And we don't want to shoot you. Don't be a fool. This is crazy stuff here. You know it is."

"Well that's me, isn't it?" cried Rory suddenly. "The crazy one. That's why they kept injecting me, isn't it, at my old school? Not like here. They let me be myself here, and I've got better, too. They like me now! Don't you, Sam?"

"Yeh, Rory, we do. Course we do. And you're not crazy. So please, drop it… Rory…"

"But maybe I am crazy, Sam! Because I've realised I like this school, after all, and I like it here on the island. I don't want it to change. I don't want to leave. I want things to keep getting better."

"Nothing will get better, son, while you have a gun in your hand," said Hammond, and he took a step closer, while Rory shuffled back, still pointing the gun, the wind brushing his hair across his face.

"You're right!" he yelled, and bent his elbow, turning the gun away from them and resting it, still shaking, against the side of his own head.

"No!" cried his mother.

"No," whispered Lia, as Millie held her arm.

"That won't help anyone either, son," said Hammond, and Sam heard something in his voice that was no longer so sure of itself.

Because of course this was worse. Rory could never have hurt any one of those men with their target training, their instant reactions and their nerveless fingers on the triggers. But he could hurt himself.

"Say you'll go and leave us alone," shouted Rory, "or I'll shoot. I'll kill myself. I will. Just say you'll go and it's over, or I'll do it. I will."

Sam didn't think in that moment, any more than he ever had, when his parents couldn't let him out of their sight for fear of what he might dare to do. He just ran out towards Rory, who turned to look at him, tears starting to slip down his cheeks to his chin.

"Come on, man," he muttered. "Do you want to break Lia's heart? I thought you wanted to be a rock star. You've got to be alive for that, you know." He paused. "Well, until you've recorded some music, anyway. Then you can shoot yourself and be famous for ever."

A smile flickered across Rory's face but the tears kept trickling.

"Leave it to us, boy!" yelled Hammond. "Get out of it, go!"

But Sam stayed where he was.

"Please, Rory, please don't do it!" cried Lia, who hardly dared to look, while Millie held on tight, just in case.

"See?" said Sam. "Don't do it to her. Or your mum. Look at her! You're frightening her. You're right, we do kind of like you. We even like your songs, you dork."

He took his eyes off Rory for just a moment, to shout at the cops gathered unmoving behind him, weapons still aimed at his head.

"He's not crazy," he told them. "He's just trying to help. It's not the best idea but nobody was coming up with any others. He wouldn't hurt anyone. He used to be angry, that's all, but he's not like that any more."

He turned back to Rory.

"Are you?"

Rory shook his head, but he didn't speak. Then he dropped to his knees and laid the gun on the grass. Lia winced away, blinded, as the sun flashed from it. Sam stared at it a moment before kicking it, which hurt.

The cops moved as one to surround him, but Sam got there first, sitting down beside him, his arm round him. Lia came running, and sat on the other side, not knowing whether to try to hold his hand.

Millie stood staring down at the top of her son's red head, unable to speak, aware that he was too big now to want it ruffled in public. He would never know how frightened she had been, or how proud. As for Rory's mother, she stood stiff in her silence until her body began to shake.

"We have to take the kid," Hammond was telling Garth, who begged him to reconsider.

As they talked, Ken Fielder appeared from nowhere, and approached the police, producing an ID card from his anorak pocket.

"You're MI5?" muttered the sergeant, incredulously, raising his hand to stop his men advancing any closer on the three teenagers.

Ken backed away and kept his voice down.

"It's my fault. It's my gun. I did this to him. He's not a danger to anyone, I guarantee."

For most of the RD brothers and sisters, the conversation between Fielder and Hammond remained a private one. But Sam and Lia heard about his mission to assess the situation on the island, his neglect of his son, and his loss of faith in what he was doing there as he had begun to believe in his new identity.

"I started to try and make it real," he muttered. "I don't expect you to understand."

"It's not me you need to explain yourself to. Your spook bosses will want to hear it. I'd save it for them – and the people you conned."

Hammond had taken the gun.

He opened the barrel and with a sleight of hand that only Ken could see, declared it empty while one hard-knuckled hand closed around a tiny bullet.

"The gun wasn't loaded," he announced, loudly enough for most to hear. "I think they call it attention-seeking behaviour, but he couldn't have meant any harm. There will be no charges."

Ken nodded and mumbled thanks.

"Plenty of tablets," added Hammond, "and possibly a good kick up the backside, but no charges."

Ken Fielder shook the hand that concealed no bullets. The other slipped into Hammond's pocket for a second before he raised it to gain the attention of the crowd.

"There are other charges that remain to be answered. But I think we've probably had enough excitement to be going on with."

Oh God, thought Sam. Alive or dead?

"Michael Brown, however, may live – thanks to …Ingmar…Henrik… the medic who appears to be less of a quack than I may have assumed. What remains critical now is what the victim may have to tell us."

Those who did not know recovered from their puzzlement to allow themselves weak cheers, mostly for Sven. Sam saw Lia's delight, and wished he could share it.

"We'll leave you guys alone for a while, to get over your little melodrama. But we will be back. And my message to you remains the same. Arrests will be made – a large number of arrests – unless you take a leaf out of this young man's book, and come to your senses."

"And our message to you remains the same, as does our resolve."

Beaky! Sam and Lia didn't know how long she had been standing there.

"Then you leave us no option," Hammond told her.

"There's always a choice," said Sam.

Hammond made no reply. As he turned, and started to lead his men away, Christy returned to the piano and played the opening chords that led into a slow and intense repeat performance of "We Will Overcome."

"Will somebody kindly fill me in?" asked Beaky. "I came back for two o'clock, but I get the feeling I missed something."

Sam did see the old mobile in her hand, but he was finding it hard not to feel let down. It was like Nelson missing the Battle of Trafalgar.

She scuttled after Hammond in a way that looked less than dignified, and once he stopped, hands on hips, wearily resigned to listening, Sam could not hear beneath the singing what she had to say. And there was something, in the lift of her head and the curve of Hammond's mouth, that made him wonder.

Rainbow Dreams had got side-tracked into gentle rejoicing, Prodigal Son style, lavishing on Rory a lot of attention, some of it from Lia. He looked pale. She was telling him not to be sick over Millie's handknit jumper that wobbled down to her thighs. Millie was offering round tea. And Beaky was walking slowly back up the hill, eyes slitting and inscrutable in the brightness. And then he had lost her in the crowd.

Nothing was over. Nothing was won. Not all the guns were empty, or available for kicking. And Beaky knew it. But what else did she know?

Twenty-Five

Singing and tea drinking made way for lessons. Orders from Darius and Beaky. Learning had rarely been so quiet – and not only because Rory had been excused classes. The Fielders were sitting in a cottage full of cardboard boxes, with Millie and Dave. And Sam's imagination didn't run much further than the "Dunno" that he placed, repeatedly, in Rory's mouth, or the arm, belonging to his mother that he pictured around shoulders.

No one asked when Hammond would be back. But when Beaky missed the start of a maths lesson he knew something extra-curricular was going on. It was only when he realised that the quiet was in part due to the absence of dog barks that he began to suspect.

"No animals," he whispered to Lia, who couldn't help enjoying the open-ended problem solving and took a while to register when she looked around her.

"Where are they?"

Sam shrugged his shoulders. But Beaky knew. He was sure of it.

The only numbers Sam really cared about were minutes, and without a watch they weren't so easy to count, but that didn't stop them passing, in the portakabin and on the police launch too. He had never been good at waiting. And he had no idea what he was waiting for.

It wasn't the first time a maths lesson had been interrupted from the sky. Suddenly the noise above them was harder to miss, like the glint of metal high and fast, piercing its way through cloud into sunlight, attracting all eyes to the heliplane racing through the sky towards them.

"Dad," murmured Lia.

All they needed, Sam might have said. But not everyone felt the same. Beaky's eyes were smiling.

"I'm getting too old for all this excitement," said Isabel, looking up from calculations she was relieved to abandon.

The community's oldest member couldn't see or hear the tiny plane with any great clarity but dimly caught its dazzle in the sunlight. Harry, one of the youngest, made a noise of the sort boys had been making before heliplanes and possibly before brick or glass.

Faye put her arm around her daughter Christy, whose fingers rested still on the piano keys as the last voice ebbed away on the word overcome.

The brothers and sisters were not the only people on the island who stood around to watch. The officers on the launch had turned and repositioned, some of their fingers itching close to triggers.

"Dad!" cried Lia, louder this time.

Beginning to approach the plane, she ducked the whirlwind of air, sidestepping the tunnel that would have sucked her down it.

The steps clicked down to the grass and the door opened into the stilling, quietening sunshine. The first legs, wrapped in unmistakeably pristine winter-weight tweed, stretched out and jumped down. Lia let her father embrace her before she asked him what on earth he thought he was wearing.

"I could say the same to you!" he retorted.

He looked her up and down, tugging the plaits that Christy had threaded with bright yellow wool. In a sweater, he thought, that could only be Millie's, she looked like one of them.

Behind him, appearing out of the heliplane, was someone else's father. At least, until recently that was the way he had thought of himself. Robbo ran towards him with arms up in a move he usually saved for goals only. Millie looked around anxiously for Hazel, and found her staring in motionless shock, eyes clouded with tears. Matt, who stood beside her, took her hand, then let it go and watched her walk slowly out onto the field.

"Lia, look, Lia!" Lars was calling. "Look who it is!"

Carl turned round and waited to put his arm round a slight, blond youth shorter than some of the boys in Dave's class. He was carrying a guitar case.

"No!" breathed Lia.

"Yes, in fact," contradicted her father. "Will, this is my daughter. Lia, meet Will. You might recognise him from the posters on your bedroom wall."

"Dad!" protested Lia, smiling shyly.

"The rest of them are in there too," Will told her.

He looked back to grin at the other band members spilling out down the steps, the drummer stumbling and needing a hand from the keyboard player.

"Not that hard to fall, then," remarked Sam to Lars.

"Oh ha very ha," he snorted.

To most of the others the joke would have meant nothing, as did the faces. But they were very familiar to the three fans who loved their music. Or perhaps there were five of those, judging by the smiles on the faces of Kara Lane and Christy, who didn't feel old enough yet to be indifferent to real live rock stars ambling towards them across the school field.

There was some confusion among the older members of the community, and the names being bandied about included Tart In The Hall and the equally mysterious Hard As A Ball. But in some form the news must have made it to the Fielders' cottage, because Rory was running towards the action. Eager, thought Sam, to put himself in the centre of it as usual.

The last two people down the steps were a man and a woman who held a soundcamera and a microphone.

"She does The News," said Rory to Sam. "I've seen her in war zones."

"So you nearly made the ten o'clock bulletin," grinned Sam. "Ten minutes earlier and you'd have been a T.V. star."

Rory was grateful for every one of those minutes. When he made his panoramoscreen debut he intended it to be for a very different reason. One day he'd be as famous as Will, the short but apparently swoonfest singer and lead guitarist with the country's coolest young band. He was already taller and just as good-looking.

Carl reassured Lia that this time he was here as an observer only. As a dad. And as a friend who wanted to help if he could. He brought a letter from Roz, inside which she found a new filmocard of Charlie.

In it, Lia saw and heard him trying to say her name for the first time, as his mum held her favourite pyjamas and let him grab them with eager hands. Lia's smile couldn't get any wider without turning into an impression of a certain police sergeant. She showed it to Sam.

Meanwhile the prize-winning BBC news reporter was introducing herself.

"I'm Gita Smith-Patel. We heard there was a situation we should be bringing to the attention of people on the mainland. Carl Harding here thinks our presence could give you some protection, should you need it."

"Will it stop them making multiple arrests?" wondered Garth.

He filled Gita in on most of the day's developments. He failed to mention an impulsive and misguided gesture with a loaded gun, and left aside the little matter of MI5 involvement. After all, they were both of them distractions and best forgotten.

"Let's see if Sergeant Hammond will explain his intentions to camera," said Gita.

She very much doubted whether he would in fact want to come out of the police launch where some of the officers had regrouped, while others appeared to be in the linegraders' portakabin.

"If you want a spokesperson who'll make great T.V, I recommend the schoolmarm with the nose," Carl Harding told her, "and the opinionated girl with a jackass for a dad."

At the school all kinds of home-baked temptations were on offer. It wasn't even a mealtime, but most of those who hadn't been very hungry seemed to have recovered their appetites.

"Ever heard the phrase eating us out of house and home?" Dave asked Carl.

"Sorry. Is that what we're doing – again?"

Carl swallowed the last filling mouthful of scone.

"You know, Dave, I owe you an apology. You had misgivings, and you turned out to be right."

"It gave me no satisfaction."

"No, I guess not. But I'm sorry. I had no idea that my little film would lead to this."

"Don't give yourself too much credit. We couldn't hide indefinitely. It couldn't have been long before somebody remembered we were here. So I guess this was waiting to happen," Dave told him. "But there's a woman whose life got turned upside down by your attempts at a balanced picture. I don't suppose sorry will cover it."

He glanced over to a corner where Robbo's recently extended family sat quietly, less interested than most in food.

"Guess not, no," said Carl, "but I'd better try."

Dave sighed and turned away as he headed in their direction. He still didn't like Carl much. But give him credit: he was doing his best to repair the damage. Coming back had taken guts. He did wonder, though, how much he'd done it for them and how much for Lia. A father would do anything to earn back the love of a daughter like that.

Dave kept looking down to the portakabins for a glimpse of red hair.

Gita was talking to the editors of the early evening News programme. It was the extended one that allowed time for reports with what they called human interest. She was hoping that in view of Carl's nomination for a BAFTA, and the recent T.V. debate about the linegraded programme, they might be given a slot.

It was the best part of the job, really: wake-up calls. But sometimes she thought New Britain had sleeping sickness.

In the launch at the jetty, Al Hammond was looking back on a day that had started so well, a day when he took the upper hand from those hippies only to lose it. He'd be more than happy to just start the engine and speed back full tilt to the mainland.

At least they hadn't had to shoot the boy, but he didn't relish trying to arrest that Bird woman in front of the cameras, and there was no knowing what those other kids might try. These media people never knew when to butt out and leave them to do their job. And then when they'd stirred things up, he'd be left to take the flak.

He would not have been best pleased if he'd seen the rock band his own daughter raved about, rehearsing an acoustic version of the song she kept humming round the house.

Nor would he have been encouraged by the commotion around the piano as Christy went into labour, suddenly and dramatically. With no Sven. There was now the imminent prospect of more lawbreaking, in the form of an illegal home birth – without the benefit of technology, pan pipes or disinfected air.

"What's the date?" asked Lia, when she realised what was going on.

"Why?" asked Sam.

"We'll need to remember it. It'll be historic."

But a historic victory or defeat? Sam didn't like to point out that the day hadn't finished yet, and they didn't know how any of it would end.

Meanwhile, Faye, the baby's grandmother and a stalwart defender of natural birth, was also thinking about dates. This wasn't the right one, the one Christy had calculated. It was much too soon. Much more frightened than she let her daughter see, she just kept praying. And still no sign of Sven.

"Mum..." Christy began.

"I know, love. Too many people."

Rock singers, reporters and men who arrived in space age planes wearing ridiculous thousand pound suits! And if there was ever a time for peace....

"Can I help?" asked the deep and unexpected voice of Debs Fielder. "I trained as a nurse."

"Oh please," said the baby's grandmother. "Please."

Debs agreed that Christy was entitled at least to a little privacy, but she had odd ideas about where she wanted to find it. One word to Beaky and the area around the Wendy House was evacuated.

"That'll do," said Debs, timing contractions. "She's comfortable. It's homely."

Faye wasn't sure that the well-used cushions looked as clean as any hospital would have liked, and wouldn't care to identify the stains. As Christy crouched on all fours, concentrating on her breathing, Faye busied herself moving chewed and dribbly toys and worn old teddies. Five weeks too soon!

It was a while since the nurse had had to deliver a baby, but she was sure that it was not the kind of skill you forgot if you didn't practise. But she was relieved when the mother managed to tell her between contractions that those five weeks were phantom.

"It's okay," she reassured Garth and Faye. "Your daughter is trying to tell you," she explained, "that she falsified her dates, in order to bend the law and have the baby here at Rainbow Dreams. The child is bang on time. Or will be, very soon."

Faye almost cried with relief. It would be alright after all.

In fact, the baby's timing proved to be close to perfect. Only minutes before Gita presented a live broadcast on the BBC News at Six, Philip Peace Hope entered the world. He was chunky, healthy and loud, and in the absence of a battery of tests, he was awarded straight A stars and pronounced beautiful.

The cheers travelled down to the kabins and beyond, as far as the deck of the police launch by the jetty, while Beaky gathered everyone to give thanks for his safe arrival.

In the silence that followed, the community committed Philip Peace Hope into the hands of the God of love. It was something Sam felt able to do with more feeling when his mother appeared with Sven to join in. The tension had cleared from their faces, and his mother's tears were a kind he recognised. They weren't the kind she'd cried on the beach with his father's body. They were the kind she'd cried when the seawater had gushed from his own throat and he'd opened his eyes.

"Under control?" asked Carl who'd slipped outside.

Gita was communicating with Television Centre for the last time before she went live.

She nodded, skimming her notes once more. Out of the corner of her eye she saw Sergeant Hammond striding towards her. He stood, hands on hips and a long way short of happy – even when he saw the baby wrapped in the towel in Christy's arms.

"I would like to advise you before you begin," said Beaky, one hand raised, "on the inappropriateness at this point of references to legal irregularities, and recommend simpler words, the kind people all over the world can still relate to – like congratulations."

Hammond stared, eyes squeezed in concentration, while Gita wished the camera were running already. The slow grin that followed made her glad it was not.

Carl felt an arm slip through his as Lia appeared with Sam.

"You ready?" he asked her.

Lia nodded. Sam gave her a warm, confident smile. The last of the day's sunlight remained, a little thin, but still warm enough to supply a glow that would make the grass greener and the sky bluer in people's living rooms.

Gita was counting down silently with her fingers. As the last one went down and the cameraman nodded, they waited for the intro from the studio in their earpieces. Though the observers couldn't hear it, the alertness on the two faces told them when it had begun.

"The school behind me," began Gita, turning her head towards it, "is the centre of the Rainbow Dreams Community featured recently in a documentary which highlighted the fact that this is the only school in Britain that has not yet been linegraded."

She paused, counting, while a clip from the film reminded viewers in their homes of a scene from the classroom that did not, Carl promised, feature Rory. Then she began again.

"Soon after the film was shown, the Department of Linegraded Education sent a unit to the island to begin a Level Three restructuring of the tiny school with its thirty-six pupils and four members of staff." Many of the thirty-six pupils seemed keen to make themselves visible.

"But as you can see if you look behind me, the brothers and sisters of Rainbow Dreams had other ideas. They have occupied the school for three days, preventing Decca Quinn and her team from entering or beginning their task. Decca, you must be frustrated, but do you have any sympathy at all for the islanders and their cause?"

"Well," began Decca, caught out by the wording, "their reasons just aren't good enough to halt progress. They'd keep us all in caves eating mammoth stew."

Sam heard a derisive laugh which had to be Rory's.

"You have a job to do," finished Gita, turning to the other side of her. "Now Decca mentioned reasons, and there is a young lady beside me who understands those reasons better than most. Lia Harding attends a flagship Level One linegraded academy in London. Lia, tell us, as a pupil, why you support this campaign."

"This is a happy school," said Lia. "People laugh here. There's no pressure. Nobody keeps telling the kids whether they're achieving their objectives, and they're not graded twenty-four seven."

The sun was unexpectedly warm on her face, but she was shivering.

"Are you telling us that linegraded education is a miserable way to learn?"

"Yes, because it shuts kids down. It breaks their spirit. Rainbow Dreamers want their children to learn to be free."

Lia saw, as the camera swung away from her, that she had done her bit. Sam gave her a thumbs up and Rory blew her a cheeky kiss which Sam couldn't help noticing.

"So we've heard why the community is so determined to preserve their school the way it is. But when the law is being broken, however playfully and peacefully, it's the job of the police to enforce it." Gita turned to Hammond

"Sergeant Hammond, that's what you were sent here to do. I understand you delivered an ultimatum to the protesters earlier today?"

Gita had hoped he would hold back the grin. It might put the nation off its supper.

"I had to inform them," he said, slowly, as if he'd practised, "that unless they vacated the school, so that the guys could get on with their task, there would be arrests."

"And when you talk of arrests, I understand you mean the teachers and governors who say they are responsible for the school."

"The ring-leaders, yes."

As he spoke, the camera panned across the faces of Millie, Beaky, Garth and Dave. They weren't quite smiling, but at that moment they were closer to it than Sergeant Hammond could manage to be.

"Tell us about the criminal charges faced by the people here," said Gita. "I understand essential components were dug into vegetable gardens?"

"Yes. That was theft."

"And that some of the panelling intended for computer cubicles was used creatively to make shelters in the open-air church?"

As he confirmed that, "Yes, this was more theft. In fact, criminal damage, also," footage from the morning was slotted into the live broadcast.

It showed the nation a brief but sunlit image of Christy and Faye, before the birth, sitting and praying in the painted shelter.

"And I gather there was also illegal interference with the central computer," Gita continued, providing the segue into a shot of the screen, with its rainbow and Rory's song. "But the people here tell me they would like to know whether there are any other charges you wish to make."

Hammond smiled one of his slow-burning smiles, which was for a moment the only thing to fill a thickening silence.

"No further charges."

The cheer that went up smothered the two additional words that he attempted to offer the microphone as Gita withdrew it. But Sam was confident they weren't love or peace.

"As we leave you," said Gita, "the situation is unresolved. But the police ultimatum was not all that was delivered here today. A premature baby, born naturally and illegally, as I'm sure Sergeant Hammond is aware, became the youngest Rainbow Dreamer to occupy the school. As you can see, Philip Peace Hope is happy to be here to support the cause – which his family believe is about preserving his future."

The proud grandmother looked down as he yawned very appealingly right on cue, to a ripple of laughter.

"Also earlier today, a heliplane made another delivery, bringing celebrity support in the shape of rock band Harder to Fall."

Will and his mates waved to the camera.

"But will it be enough to save the school from a change which conflicts with the values of this community? Time, as they say, will tell. This is Gita Smith-Patel for the BBC, at Rainbow Dreams."

In the last two seconds before the transmission ended, a new, unusually rhythmic version of We Will Overcome began. Joining in with the band was a young musician previously seen using a guitar in a less creative context, who made just a flicker of an appearance on the national news.

Gita turned to Beaky and shook her hand. They moved further away from the music, which was becoming rockier and more rousing by the minute.

"I'm so sorry, Mrs Bird, we ran out of time."

"No need to apologise. There's nothing I could have said that my friend didn't say better," she assured her, smiling warmly at Lia and putting a bony arm round her shoulder.

"What happens now?" asked Millie, noticing that Hammond had made a hasty exit. "They won't be back to arrest us, will they?"

"If they do," said Gita. "It'll be on camera. There will be shots of young mums and grandmothers being dragged away from their families."

"They won't, though, will they? They won't dare, not now?" cried Lia, unable to bear the thought of it, picturing Christy being torn away from poor illegal Philip Hope.

Millie hugged her but they couldn't promise anything; nobody could. And Lia's father seemed to have learned not to try.

"Thanks for coming, Dad," she told him, and they stood and joined in the song.

"I always liked a party," he said, and jigged and clapped beside her.

"Don't," she told him. "It's embarrassing."

Carl smiled, but it was too late to stop now. His legs had a life of their own. Besides, Kara Lane was an extraordinary mover; it would be unchivalrous to leave her without a partner. Lia rolled her eyes at Sam, who shook his head in pity.

Beaky, who loved Puccini and Bach rather better than she could ever love Harder to Fall, had watched long enough. Remembering ancient words woven into another song from a different age, that there is, amidst the seasons as they turn, a time to dance, she decided that this must be it.

Twenty-Six

A long day was not yet over. Gita heard from her BBC bosses that other channels wanted footage, and the papers were asking for movieshots. Her own editors were making room for a shortened version, plus a quick update, on the late evening bulletin. She invited Beaky to have the final word this time.

By nine o'clock the darkness, thicker than the mainlanders ever knew it at home, was lit only by a fire outside and candles in the corridors. Most of the children were asleep, and the singing, worn away like the fire, had faded from roaring choruses to wispy solos curling up quietly into the night air.

Beside the fire a large group remained. As well as songs, poems were recited. Lia tried to offer from memory *Everyone Sang* by Siegfried Sassoon, her favourite poem ever and one that seemed to belong to the day. When it slipped away from her, halfway through, Beaky prompted her and they finished it together.

And Millie, memories stirred by events in the Wendy House, asked Will if he knew a very old song by Nina Simone. She had to help him with some of the words, but there were others he seemed to know amazingly well, and as he declared that he'd got his freedom, he'd got LIIIIFE, tears trickled down her cheek.

"You okay?" whispered Dave, passing her a drink she hadn't made for a change.

She nodded, and took his hand.

There were times when Beaky felt as old as her reflection, but there were moments too, like the one just past, when she knew her heart was no older than Lia's. Besides, she had always tried to understand young people, and she intended to keep trying, long after her job came to an end, one way or another. Watching the boy sing, she reminded herself that it didn't matter that he wasn't pitch perfect and had no technique. He had passion, and passion blew the rest away.

While Will sang Nina Simone, there was an unusual level of activity in the portakabins. Lulu, who had a baby at home herself, had asked Carl a favour and he was happy to oblige. His pilot was on standby to take the band back to London anyway, and was there in an hour to take the linegraders with him.

There was room too for one other passenger, who needed to hand in his resignation with his gun, before his bosses could get in first and dismiss him.

"Say it now then," Rory told his father, in the doorway of the cottage. "I don't want everyone seeing what crap you are at goodbyes."

Ken had already said sorry, but for the moment Rory didn't know what to do with it. Neither of them could remember the last time they'd hugged and Rory hoped he wouldn't try it because he wasn't ready, not yet. They left the cloudy eyes to Debs, who took Rory's arm as his father turned away, but couldn't hold it. He walked. Nothing to see. Nothing he wanted to feel.

The islanders promised to dismantle the portakabins and look after the contents until the DOLE saw fit to use or reclaim them. A small crowd watched the coloured lights disappear like a firework into the darkness.

"They weren't really the enemy, were they?" said Rory, emerging from the shadows. "Not like Sharkface."

"Sergeant Hammond speaks very highly of you," Dave told him.

He put his arm round Rory's shoulder a moment, but knew not to leave it there for long.

"Maybe," he added, "he'd find it easier to walk in our shoes than we would in his."

"Not in yours, he wouldn't," Rory objected, nose wrinkling in disgust.

On the other side of the school, Gita was in a quiet corner with the cameraman, who held a torch so that she could scribble as she listened. The earlier report had generated a lot of what her editor in London called heat. Human interest, controversy, nostalgia, a baby! It was all there, and it seemed people felt strongly.

Rarely, her boss told Gita, could he remember such consensus among viewers. The responses coming in from the chilled and plugged-in homes of New Britain could be summarised in three simple words: Leave them alone. And the many ae mails and calls with a message for Sergeant Hammond could be distilled into one.

Go.

What he didn't know, and couldn't tell her, was that the same single word message had found its way to the officers on the police launch where Mikey Brown was making up for his long silence with a detailed story punctuated by vain requests for beer.

Hammond didn't want to hear it again – the secret booze store he didn't want to share (fat schmuck) swigged on the bleakest northern tip of the beach, till he tripped and fell. The concussion in the dark. The bad luck that washed him into the only cave on the island big enough to hide him.

Linegraded education or precious little education at all, in Hammond's book, it made precious little difference. The world was overrun by idiots. Okay, he couldn't lay that title at the doc who'd saved Mikey, or the woman with the nose who'd been a lady, but the red-haired kid had been pretty damned stupid, risking his life for a head-case, a loser if ever he saw one. And he'd seen plenty.

It wasn't that Hammond hadn't got the message. He'd heard it enough times to recognise the sight and sound of it. It was more a matter of a different message that he needed to pass on to the community, one that was best saved until the cameras had left. A twist. A sting. A not to be underestimated reminder. And yes, payback too, of a kind.

The live broadcast, which was the last item before the sport, was less dramatic than the editors might have liked. But the fire and the candles made an atmospheric backdrop.

"Since my last report before twilight fell here at Rainbow Dreams," continued Gita, after the viewers had been shown clips from the six o'clock programme, "the situation has changed.

First, at about eight, Decca Quinn and her DOLE colleagues withdrew by heliplane to await further orders. Now I understand that Sergeant Hammond and his officers are also preparing to leave."

Rory whooped and Sam came in on the end of it. The camera picked out faces around the fire.

"The islanders are taking a breather right now, but there's been a lot of singing here tonight. Nobody is talking of victory yet. But I have to say there's a real sense of peace and unity here."

The microphone was in front of Beaky now.

"The last word for tonight comes from Indira Bird, widow of one of the original founders of this community, and teacher for more than thirty five years at the school behind us."

"Best teacher in the history of the universe!" yelled Henry's nine-year-old sister, who rarely said an uninvited word in her lessons but often made Beaky cards that were labours of love.

"Hooray!" called just about everyone else.

"Mrs Bird, as you see, is a very popular teacher and one whose creativity and ability to inspire her pupils would, of course, be sacrificed to linegraded education. Indira, can I ask you for your feelings this evening? Is it over?"

"Well, it's rather late in my career," said Beaky, "for me to begin to understand the great minds that dictate what education is, or should be. But my feelings are a different matter. I feel

242

proud of the stand we have made, and of the courage and faith of the young people who have made it possible."

She paused, the camera catching the light in her eyes as she smiled at Lia and Sam.

"And if you ask me, is it over, my answer is yes. My brain tells me it could be, and my heart feels it has to be. But I also hope that it's only just begun."

"This is Gita Patel-Smith for the BBC, at Rainbow Dreams."

For all her boniness, Beaky had not gone short of hugs over the years, but she had never quite been mobbed before.

Within twenty minutes the recently returned heliplane had taken Gita and her cameraman back to London, along with an increasingly talkative Mikey Brown heading for hospital in Greatport. But Carl Harding caved in under pressure from his daughter and agreed to stay a little longer. It would give him the chance to see her riding bareback on Shadow, and get to know a little better all the people he had only really known as characters in his own scenes.

And Indira Bird was one of them – the one whose phone call had persuaded him to humour his demanding daughter one more time, use contacts, and take a shot at redemption at the same time. But when Sam and Lia saw the two of them chatting, they overheard two words on the end of a sentence from Beaky that Sam had not quite heard before, from a toothier mouth.

"Not yet."

They stared at each other.

"It isn't finished, is it?" Lia whispered, and Sam, who had no words, shook his head as he held her hand.

Twenty-Seven

People were tired, suddenly, and the elation of victory reshaped into something softer, stiller, a glow in silence like a fire allowed to rest. Some of the families were asking to go home.

"Not, I think," Beaky told them, "until Hammond does the same."

"Surely…" began Faye, but stopped, because she had known Indira Bird for a very long time, been a tiny bridesmaid for her and Tom, and sharpened her mental maths in her classroom.

Darius O'Dell thought it wasn't like Beaky to be a wet blanket dampening spirits she herself had helped to raise.

"They'll be gone soon," said Dave. "Nothing left to stay for. Tails between their legs."

"Let's hope so, yes," said Beaky, but her smile was straight, and short.

As evening darkened into night the islanders gathered in the hall for one more night.

"What is he waiting for?" Lia asked Sam, looking out in the twilight towards the jetty where look-outs reported that the boat had not moved.

"To save face? To enjoy the power to scare us a little bit longer?"

"Ah," said Beaky, overhearing, "but the power he thinks he holds is the product of his own imagination."

The smile, wider now, should have reassured Sam. He wanted it to. With no idea of sleeping, he found and unfolded his blanket. Rory and his mother, who had spent a lot of time together since Ken left, had arrived, several paces apart. Sam hadn't had a chance, hadn't had the guts, to talk to him, since...... Rory looked pale, but then the light was faint, art house, his face like a photograph. The kind a girl might want on a wall.

Sam watched as Lia walked over to him, touched his arm, said something short, and quiet. Something that changed the photograph, the mood, the light. But what? He had no right to ask, if she did not want to tell him.

Sam knew he would not sleep, shuffled off to the kitchen to look for food, and found he wasn't hungry either. When he returned to the hall Rory was singing "We will overcome" as some kind of end of twentieth century rap, complete with moves, in a feeble attempt at a whisper that acknowledged those who slept.

Lia placed a hand across his mouth. He grabbed it and for a moment Sam thought he was going to kiss it like a Jane Austen hero. But she was too quick for him.

"Indira! Darius!"

The door was ajar to allow the islanders to settle by moonlight. Dave's whisper came through it from a still night outside.

"Hammond."

His torch threw a wide, glaring beam that swept ahead of him, dazzling children who had already closed their eyes inside. The hall was alive again, if not fully awake. Smaller beams in a pattern of light bounced in and out of formation as other officers followed behind him. Sam counted. Two missing. But from what he could see, the boat was in darkness down on the moonlit water.

Beaky was out there already to greet him. Everyone followed, Sam pulling on jeans out of which he had already slid as he hopped from one leg to another. Lia ran, close behind Beaky, with Rory bare-chested behind her, carrying something.

"Thank you" said Beaky, as Hammond shone the glare away from their eyes and around their ankles and calves. "We appreciate the courtesy."

"Some might say you're blind enough already."

"I was referring to the courtesy of your call, to say goodbye."

A thin milky tunnel of light from Rory's torch lit up Hammond's face, but he grinned back through it.

"We are leaving, yes," he said, "but not, as you might say, empty-handed." He looked back to his men, who were hidden now, pinpoints hovering in darkness. "Right, lads?"

"Is that so?" asked Beaky, ignoring the laddish noises from the pinpoints.

"It's a question of the law," continued Hammond, "because, you see, when I find infringements of that law, however minor they might be, it is my duty to take action."

Sam didn't want to hear it. But Beaky's smile had not wavered.

"The animals on this island that you consider pets are in fact illegal, having had no anti-bacteria injections and no tests to assess the need for pharma-chilling. It is therefore my duty to ensure that these animals comply with regulations on the mainland."

"Indeed?" said Beaky. "You are, I take it, referring to the dogs and cats, one goat, and indeed, a large rabbit secreted into the heliplane not so long ago, and by now being cared for somewhere on your mainland, without the aid of drugs."

"Animals of the world unite!" cried Rory. "Cry freedom!"

Sam gaped at Lia. Beaky had done it – read his nasty mind. One step ahead as always. All the animals safe, rounded up and whisked away to safety! Go, Beaky!

"If you wish to attempt to round up the chickens, be our guests. There are thirty-seven, not one of which is likely to co-operate. We have eggs you will not find. And they hatch, you know."

"Is that right?" he said. "I wasn't a great scholar. But I think we'll overlook the chickens. Some of us married men are henpecked enough."

One or two of them laughed. Sam heard Lia mutter something about sexism and jokes that died a death in a different century.

Hammond swivelled his torch away. The light glared back towards the launch. Yes! At last! He had turned. Like a batsman no longer able to ignore the umpire's finger, he was walking. Sam looked back at Lia, wishing he could reach for her hand – before the blinding arc, a dazzle that blacked. The light was back, towering up and down, swirling around their feet.

"But you've overlooked something yourselves. Something very large. Too big to hide. And almost too big to fit into the launch."

Silence. Sam felt it like a hollowing inside.

"Took a lot of medication and all the strength my men could muster."

"No!" breathed Lia.

Sam's free hand clenched. A bead of sweat cooled icy on his forehead. Only one word filled his head and his tongue could not work it.

Shadow.

"They'll be glad to have him in the research labs, horses being rare these days. For trials." Hammond paused in the silence. "All these drugs that chill the trouble-makers have to be tested first, you know, and we can testify to the trouble that animal can make! Eh, lads?"

Grim laughter from pinpoints. A wailing cry from Philip Hope inside the school.

"Scum!"

Lia looked at Rory. But his cry was not angry. She knew it was more like the tear that she felt, hot and sharp even once she had brushed it away.

"You can't do that."

Dad! She wanted to believe him. But Hammond retorted that Carl Harding, being an inhabitant of the real world, should know he could.

"And in fact, have."

There was a grunt as Rory hurled the torch in Hammond's direction. Not so much a strike as a foot stamped, it fell to the grass far short of the bigger, brighter lights, and thudded softly.

Silence clung to the school, thick as mist, and Sam could not stand it.

"Simple courtesy, as you say, to let you know, before we leave," came Hammond's voice, no longer circled in light, since Rory's torch had fallen close to the shiny boots where it had landed. "Goodbye. It's been an education."

"What do we have to do," shouted Rory, as they reshaped the formation and faded away towards the shore. "to get the horse back?"

"Nothing," Dave told him. "It's not about that any more. We saved the school. He's saved face. His job, maybe."

"Yeah," said Rory, "but his soul's in trouble, right?"

The lights bobbed at speed. The men were in a hurry. Sam pictured them heading for the jetty, closer by the second. When the throttle kicked into life, they would be sweeping off beyond reach, with Shadow lying trapped below deck, netted, doped, his eyes closed only to open again blank as sleep without dream.

Millie's arms found him in the darkness, but they could not hold him. Snatching Rory's torch, lit up by the edge of the glare, Sam began to run. As he tore into the wind streaming off the water, he hardly cared who followed, their voices lost in his listening – for an engine, for the tug of aluminium against water.

Somewhere amidst the sounds, through the chaos of his name, repeated, overlapping and choatsed, he heard Hammond shout the order. The waves were slapping against the launch, sending a taste of spray sharp into the air he gulped as he slid and stumbled closer to the pebbles. Then they were under his feet, slipping, colliding, piling and tumbling apart. He didn't look. Like eating fire. No need to feel. No power to hold him back. He'd known them too well – back of his hand – all his life.

The milky circles of light scattered the sea as he ran, missed their target, lit up scudding cloud and rising crests, until they rested on the bright white metal breaking from the jetty, and Hammond's knuckle around the rope. Perhaps he waved, Perhaps he called goodbye. The wind and sea were swallowing the sound around him, the voices behind him calling his name.

"Shadow!" he cried.

Louder than anything else, his shout roared free as the engine settled into a whine.

"Sam! Wait for me!"

Rory. No chance. Didn't do pebbles. Or sea. Up to him. His horse, really, always had been.

"Shadow!" Sam cried again, wading on, but it was smothered by a rushing weir that foamed towards him, forced out from behind as the boat burst away. It was too late. The launch began to gather speed, the weir stretching thin into bubbles bursting feebly on pebbles. Any minute now the torchlight would lose it without trace.

Lia was breathing his name, close on the wind. But he could not see her. Nothing she could do. Nothing.

Sam turned his head, away from the sea, towards the faces moon-white in his dimming beam. Her face, lost and found. His mother's too, in her hands.

As he stopped, shivering for the first time, it juddered from behind him, faint at first, ripping through the murmur. A cry. Vibrato, nostril-wide from a barrelled chest. Metal. Tearing, breaking, bursting. The blurred and muffled beat of hooves. A shot from a gun.

"Shadow!"

Like an answer came the rearing whinny of a louder cry. Sam wheeled the torchlight towards the sound, watched it float to land on a swirl of gleaming blackness rising and kicking. Shadow was on the deck, pounding it, careering around it like a bucking bronco. And jumping.

He was in the water now. Both hands on the torch, Sam steered it wildly, but he had lost him to the waves. Without thinking he began to wade, swinging the light as he stepped in, deeper, pushing, mouth in a gasp of memory, feet forcing on through advancing waves that tried to spit at him.

"Shadow!"

It was Lia's voice, and after it came Shadow's answer, louder now. His head lifted stiff above the water, Shadow was swimming home. Like an Olympic athlete running for the tape, he made for the crowd calling his name. Nearer and nearer, the head lost and found again and again, he thrust for the beach. And for the boy chest-deep yards from it, dipping the light from his eyes.

"No more fear, boy."

It was almost a whisper. Out of the darkness he came, mane spraying, blackness heavy with shine, his knees folding and straightening to rise up steady, where Sam could reach his head.

"It's alright," Sam called weakly, addressing them all, Lia, his mother, Rory and the crowd. And Shadow too. "It's over now."

Twenty-Eight

Within twenty-four hours the Prime Minister was confirming in the House of Commons that the school at Rainbow Dreams would not be restructured, at least not in the foreseeable future. And yes, in view of the questions being asked, it was time to review the success of the first few years of linegraded education. As the government had always intended to do.

The news was delivered by the pilot of the returning heliplane, greeted by islanders stirring from sleep and bringing with him a mother anxious to see her daughter, a cat in need of the kind of attention that no one else ever lavished on her, and a toddler who really did set out to eat everything he could reach.

Lia was desperate to show her brother everything and Sam was eager to help. They were both determined that he should catch a glimpse of the dolphins. The two of them tried to enclose him between them in their quiet, patient watchfulness, but there was no holding him. When he escaped to gather noisy armfuls of tasty-looking pebbles, Lia had to scoop him up and carry him off, wriggling excitedly and pointing at everything on the way to feed the chickens.

But when they introduced him to Shadow, the close range magnificence of the huge black head silenced him into awestruck stillness.

Lia and Sam looked into the horse's eyes. Same Shadow. Light unclouded, undimmed. "A victory for resistance," Sven called him. "A miracle," said Millie.

Lia tried to widen her brother's limited vocabulary with words like heroic, regal and proud, but Charlie opted for an impression instead: of all that noisy air leaving the large, powerful nostrils. And Sam's riotous laughter was enough incentive to do it again, and again.

"Don't laugh too much!" Roz told them, when he repeated it for his parents' benefit. "He doesn't need encouraging!"

"Oh, great!" said Carl. "Snorting horse! A real cracker of a party piece to impress our guests at dinner!"

Charlie was most intrigued by Philip Peace Hope. For the moment, the newest RD brother needed a lot less attention. He lived mostly in a soft, warm world of his own, from which he surfaced only for the milk which fed him, reassured him and lulled him back to his dreams. But that didn't stop Charlie trying to touch him, and he seemed extremely pleased when his new friend stretched out his tiny hand towards his finger, albeit for a moment, before closing his eyes once more.

The next departure was something of a compromise. Ken was back, minus gun and job, but with compulsory psycho-chilling sessions booked on the mainland. He and Debs were not ready to stay and become the people they had pretended to be. But neither could they return to the people they were.

In any case, their son had always been a different matter. They knew he could not be persuaded to leave of his own free will. It was Darius who came up with a solution which meant him living on the island during school terms, with occasional visits at weekends in one direction or another across the sea.

But it was Beaky who offered him a term-time home. There would be rules, she said, that he must agree to accept, and she couldn't promise to put up with his singing in the early hours. She offered him time to think before he made up his mind, but he didn't need it.

It seemed sensible that his parents be invited to share the flight that would take the Hardings home. Three days after Rainbow Dreams made the national news, Lia and her family said goodbye to Sam and Millie, Dave and Beaky, Rory.....and everyone else assembled on the school field.

Sam stood, aware of too many arms and legs and nothing to do with them. Rory had no such difficulty. Sam could only watch as he smiled at Lia, did some kind of rock and roll swivel that should have looked ridiculous and gave her a high five.

"Don't be stupid," she said, laughing, and put her arms round his neck.

"I'll send you the debut album."

"Good. It'll come in handy if Charlie's still teething."

Sam had heard them loud and clear through the general hubbub which suddenly seemed to stop. Then Rory started to engage Dave in a conversation about the old days when music was real.

"Bye, Lia," said Sam, feeling dumb.

She knew he couldn't say what he wanted to say, because she couldn't either. It was too much, and besides, it was muddled.

"Thanks for having me," she told him, "especially as I wasn't actually invited."

He grinned.

"You never are."

She smiled.

"You'll never get rid of me, you know."

"I know."

Lia could see he wasn't going to let himself cry, but that couldn't stop her. She hugged him, in case he wasn't going to allow himself to do that either, and he held on tight.

"I love you," she said, over his shoulder, hoping the wind hadn't carried it away.

"Love you too."

In the end it was Lia who pulled away. Everyone else was talking. Did her dad never shut up, never stop charming the ladies? Rory and Dave seemed to be doing air guitar. And Charlie was crying too, much louder than she was, as if he knew how she felt.

"We'll be back," said Carl, "if you'll have us. No cameras. No dramas."

"Deal," said Dave, dignity retrieved as invisible chords made way for a firm hand to shake. "Good pitch."

Sam watched as they boarded the plane, Lia last of all. She gave him a final wave before she disappeared, still wearing the jumper which Millie wanted her to keep. Seconds later he found her face again, framed in the circular window near the front, waving quickly, then slowly, as the smile wobbled. He tried to hang on to his own, like a forced grin for a camera. As if she couldn't spot a fake a mile off!

Within a blink, that's where she was. More than a mile off. More than twenty. He would never get used to how quickly these giant silver bugs could open up a distance too massive for sight or sound to bridge.

"We'll all miss her," said Millie, as Dave took her hand. "Won't we?"

Sam managed a nod, but not, for the moment, any words.

"Someone's got to change the world," said Beaky, "and if anyone can do it, she can."

Sam said nothing as he walked back home, content to be the silent one in a noisy crowd, and save the jokes for another day. He was very tired, and happier, much happier, in spite of the sadness, than he knew how to explain.

But he couldn't help thinking that Beaky, though a very brilliant woman, had got it wrong for once about the world and Lia. She'd changed it already.